The Beginner's Guide to Being Outside

by Gill Hatcher

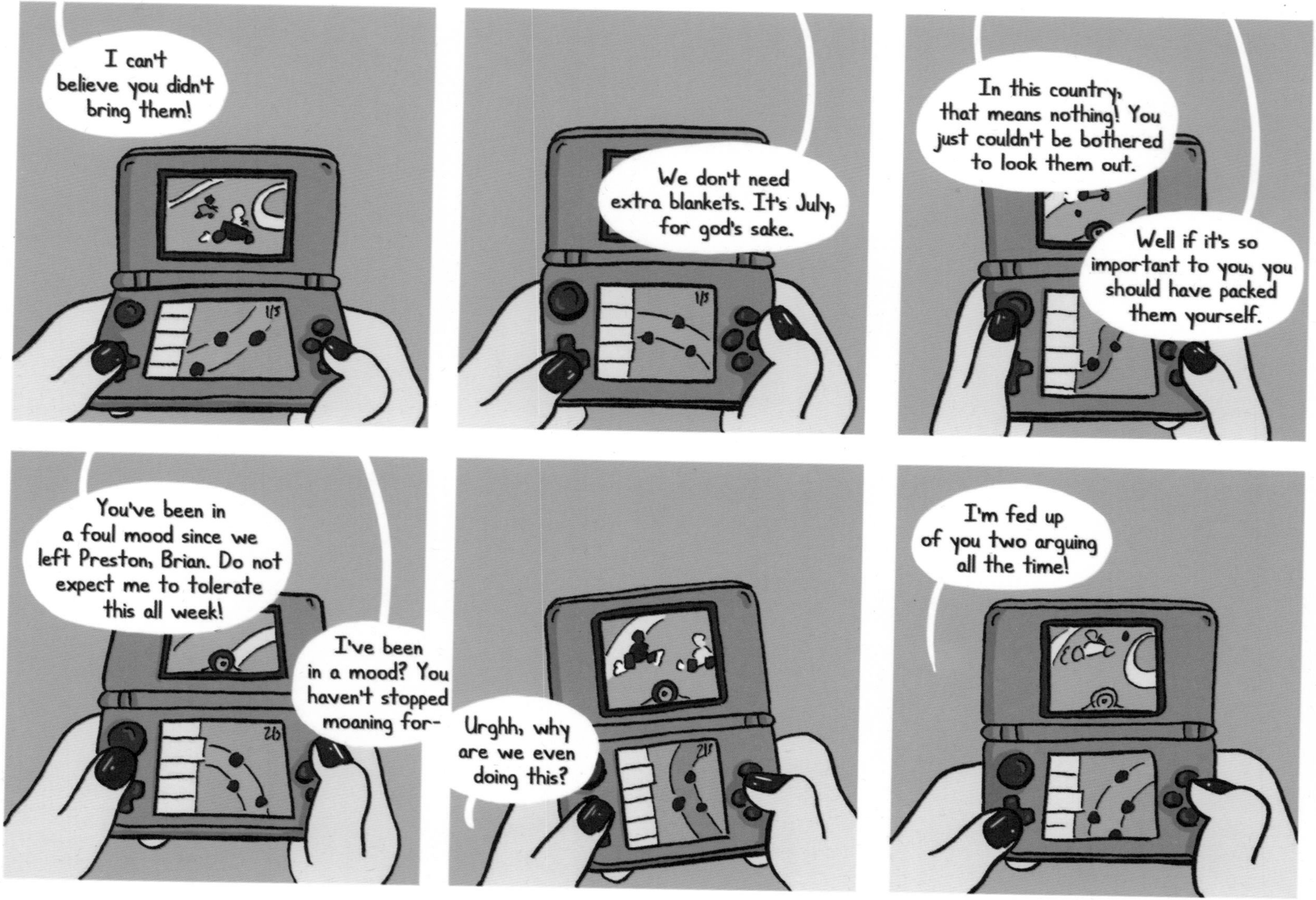
I can't believe you didn't bring them!
We don't need extra blankets. It's July, for god's sake.
In this country, that means nothing! You just couldn't be bothered to look them out.
Well if it's so important to you, you should have packed them yourself.
You've been in a foul mood since we left Preston, Brian. Do not expect me to tolerate this all week!
I've been in a mood? You haven't stopped moaning for-
Urghh, why are we even doing this?
I'm fed up of you two arguing all the time!

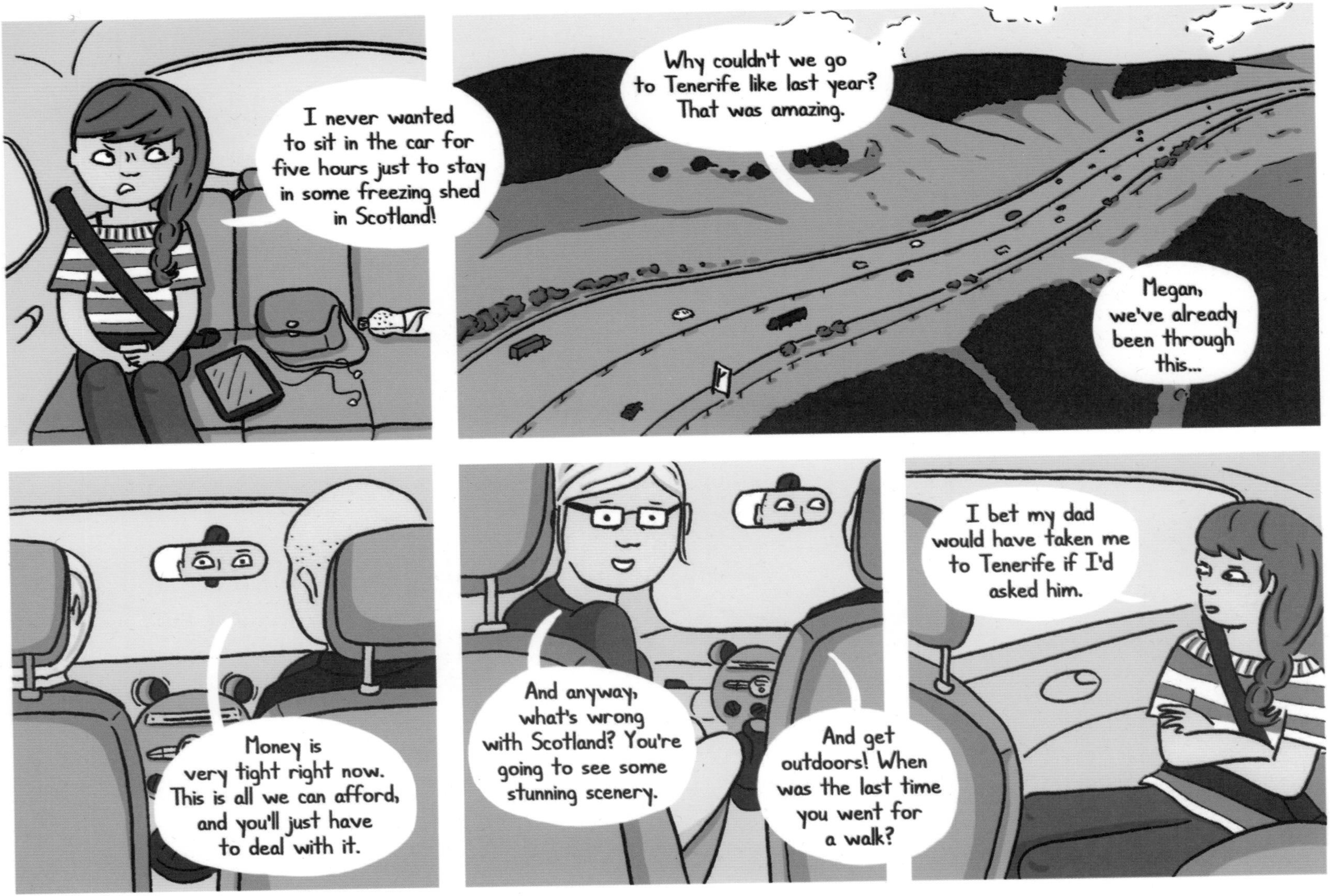

I never wanted to sit in the car for five hours just to stay in some freezing shed in Scotland!
Why couldn't we go to Tenerife like last year? That was amazing.
Megan, we've already been through this...
Money is very tight right now. This is all we can afford, and you'll just have to deal with it.
And anyway, what's wrong with Scotland? You're going to see some stunning scenery.
And get outdoors! When was the last time you went for a walk?
I bet my dad would have taken me to Tenerife if I'd asked him.

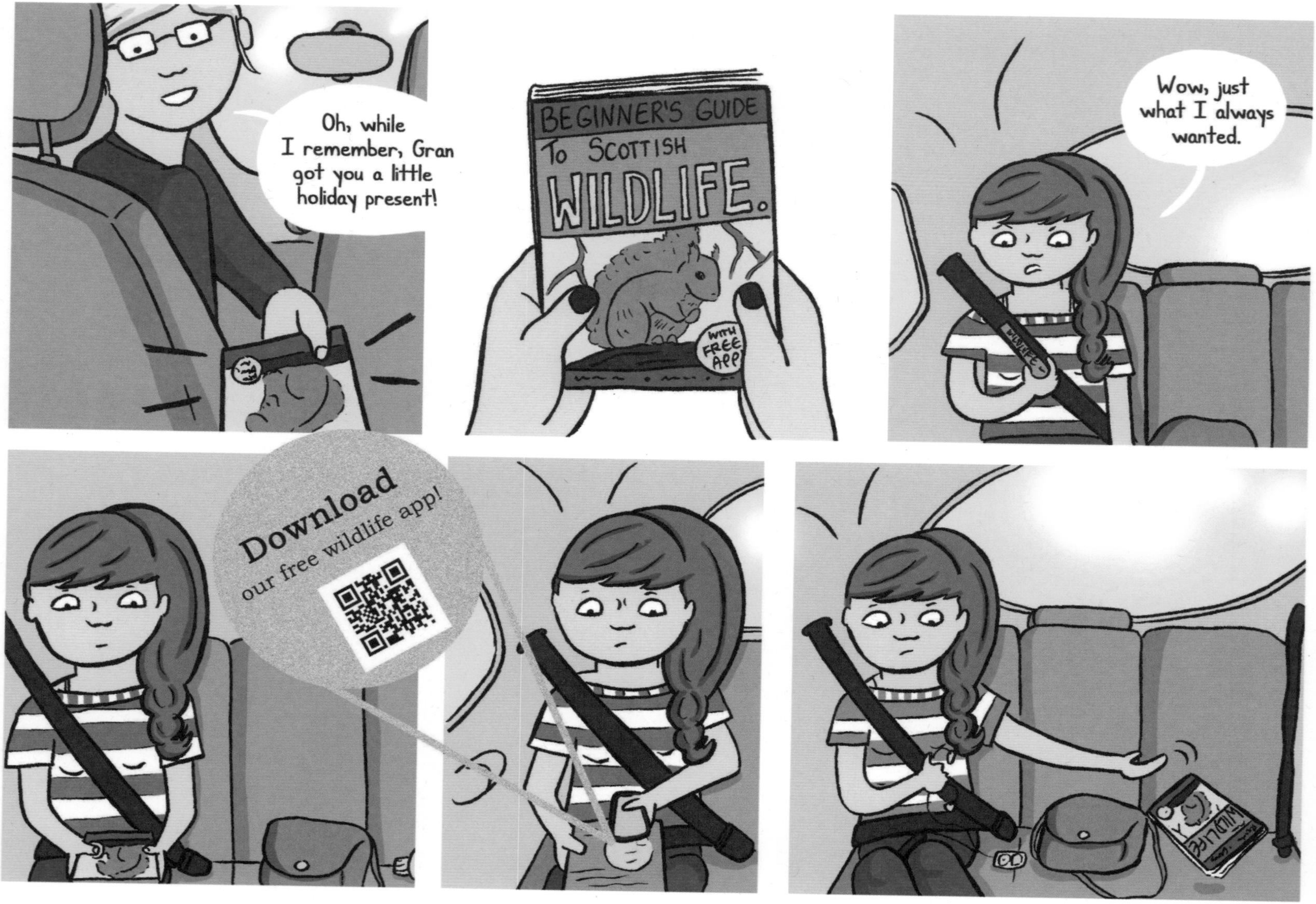
Oh, while I remember, Gran got you a little holiday present!
BEGINNER'S GUIDE To SCOTTISH WILDLIFE.
WITH FREE APP
Wow, just what I always wanted.
Download our free wildlife app!

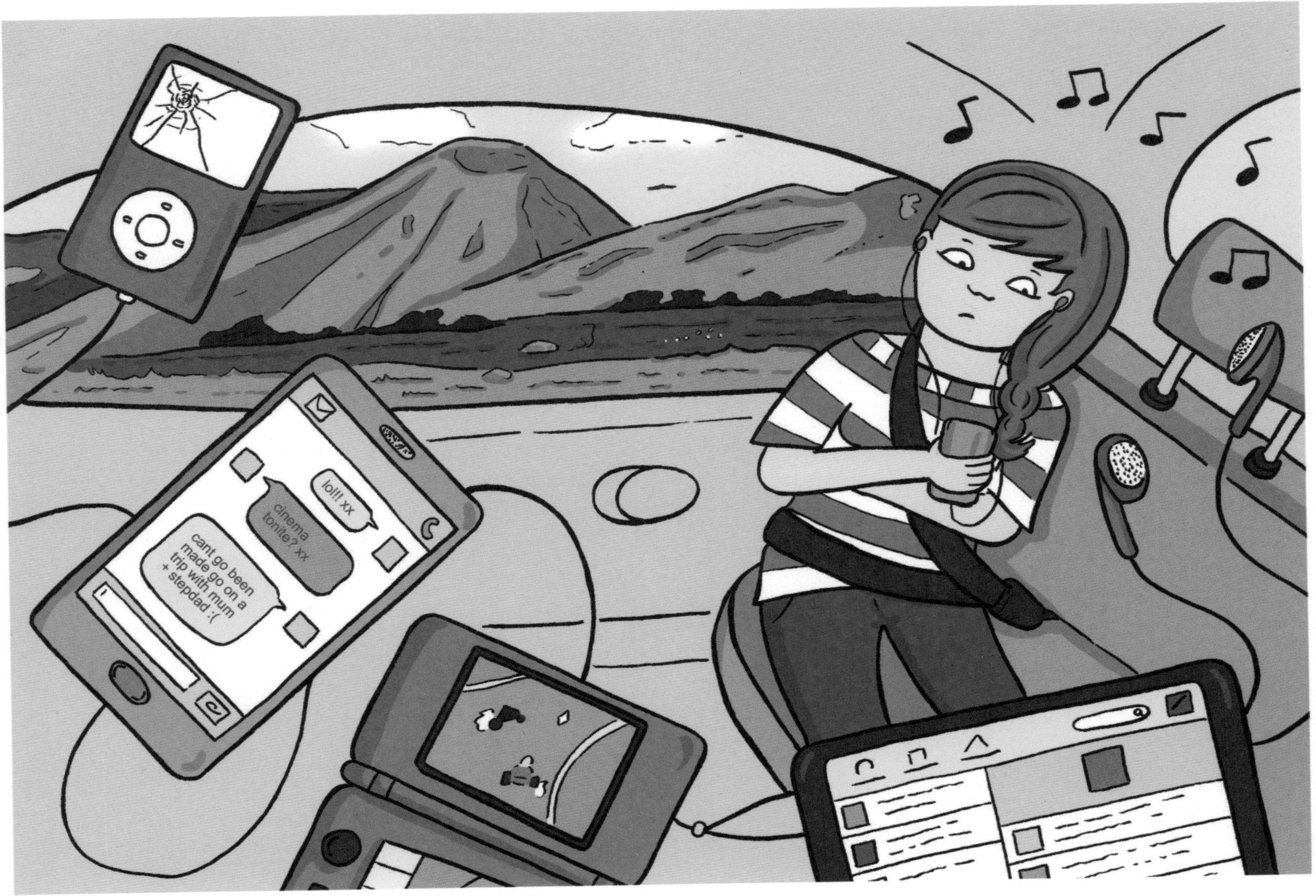
lol!! xx
cinema tonite? xx
cant go been made go on a trip with mum + stepdad :(

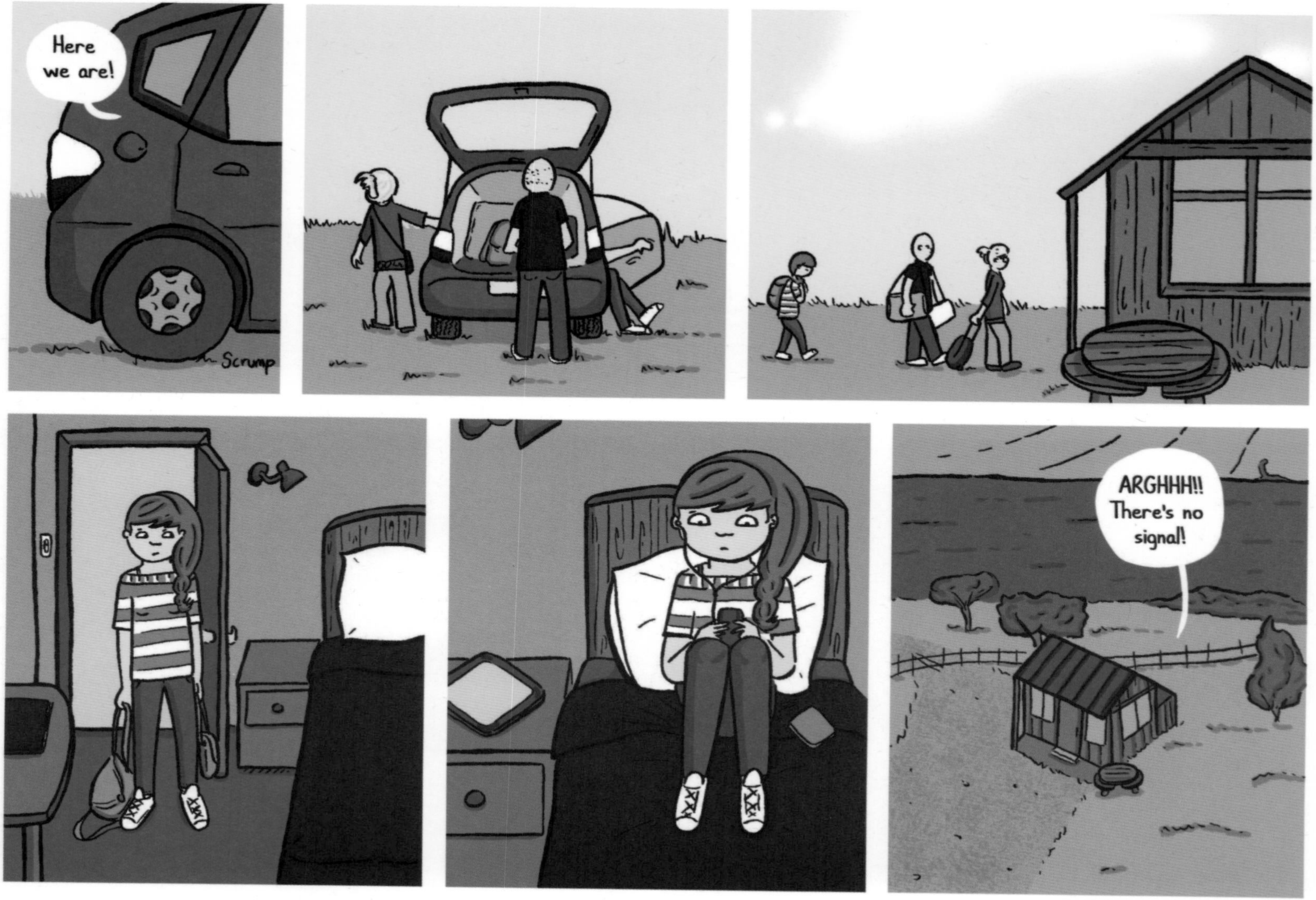
Here we are!
Scrump
ARGHHH!! There's no signal!

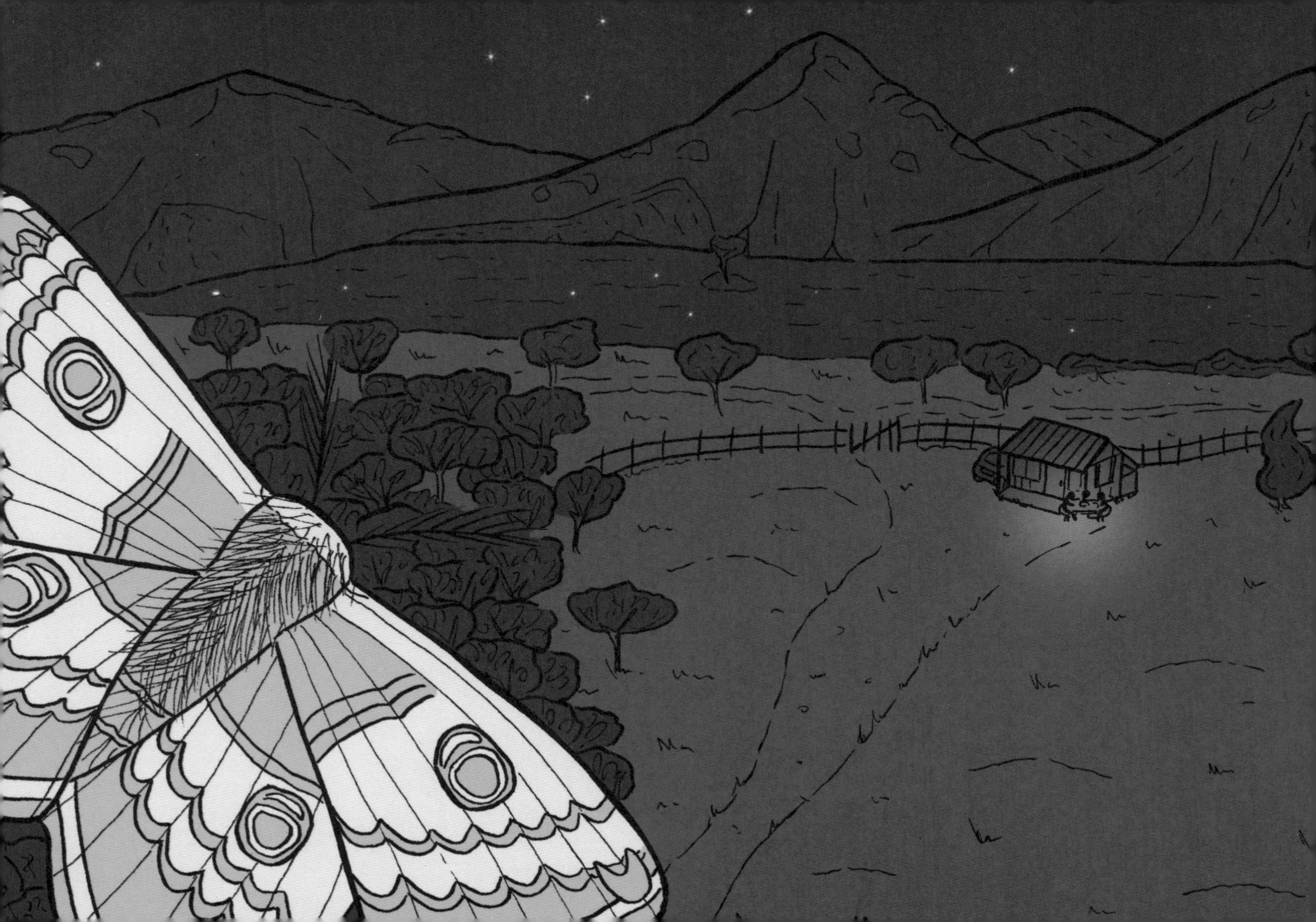

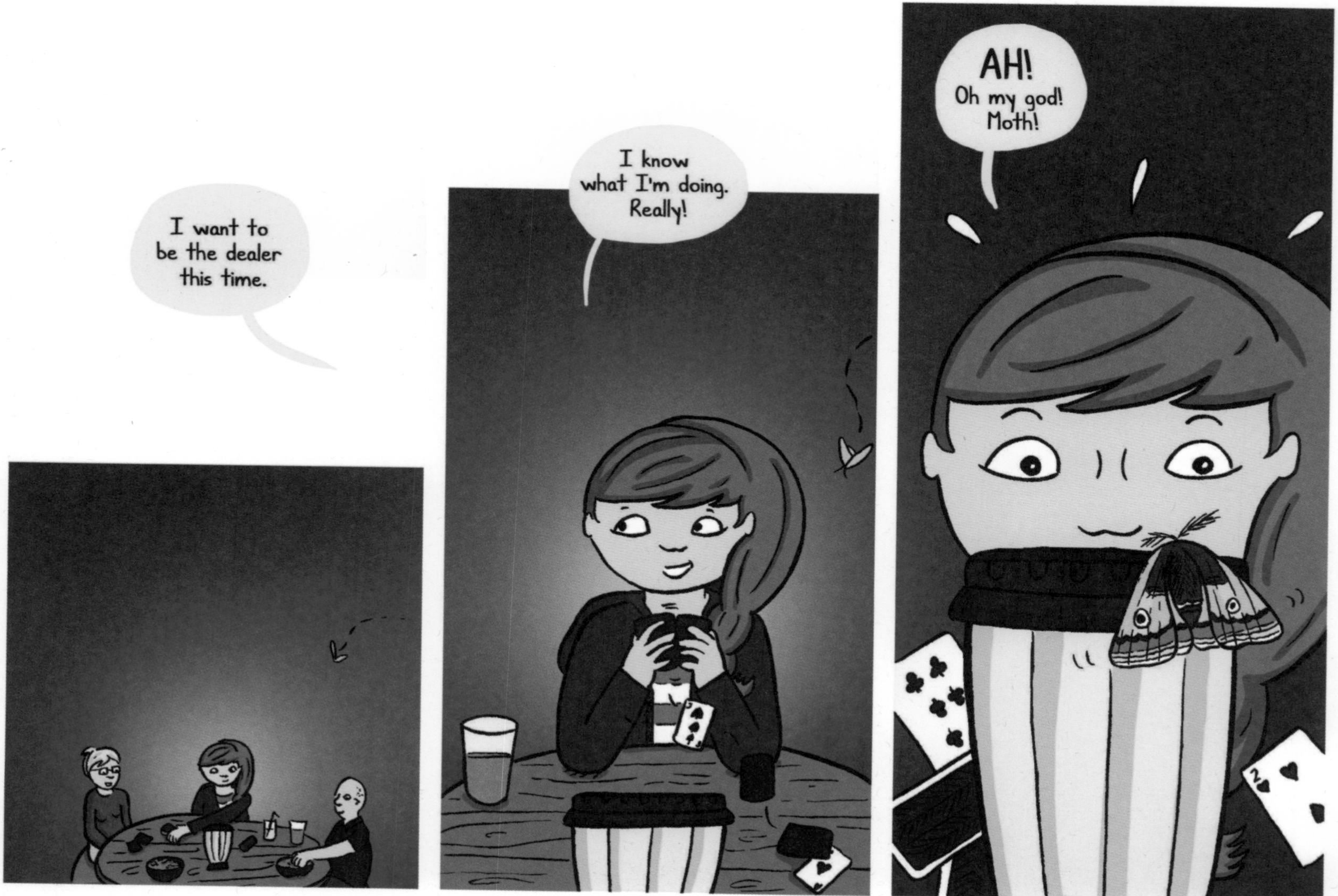
I want to be the dealer this time.
I know what I'm doing. Really!
AH! Oh my god! Moth!

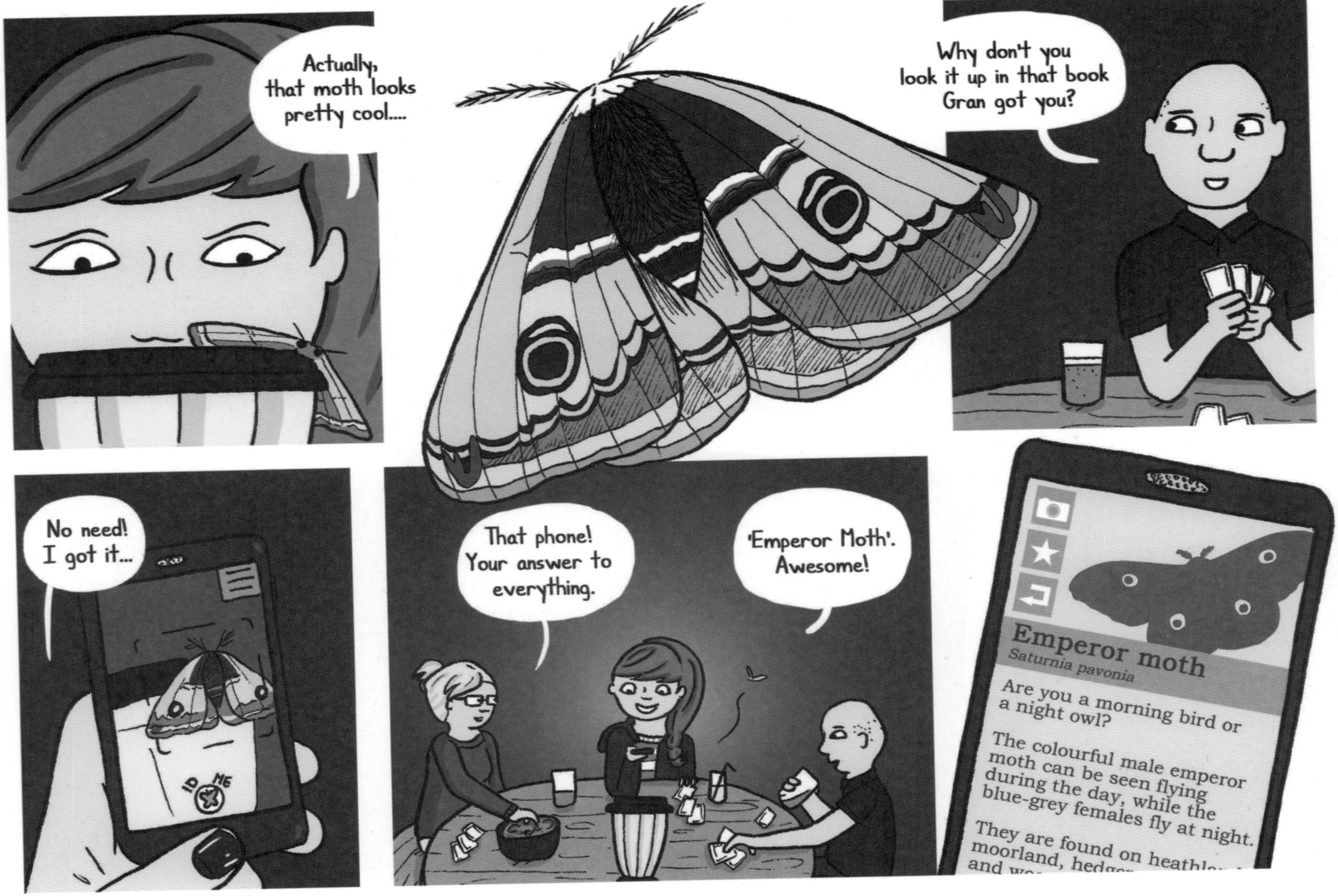
Actually, that moth looks pretty cool....
Why don't you look it up in that book Gran got you?
No need! I got it...
ID ME
That phone! Your answer to everything.
'Emperor Moth'. Awesome!
Emperor moth
Saturnia pavonia
Are you a morning bird or a night owl?
The colourful male emperor moth can be seen flying during the day, while the blue-grey females fly at night.
They are found on heathland, moorland, hedgerows and

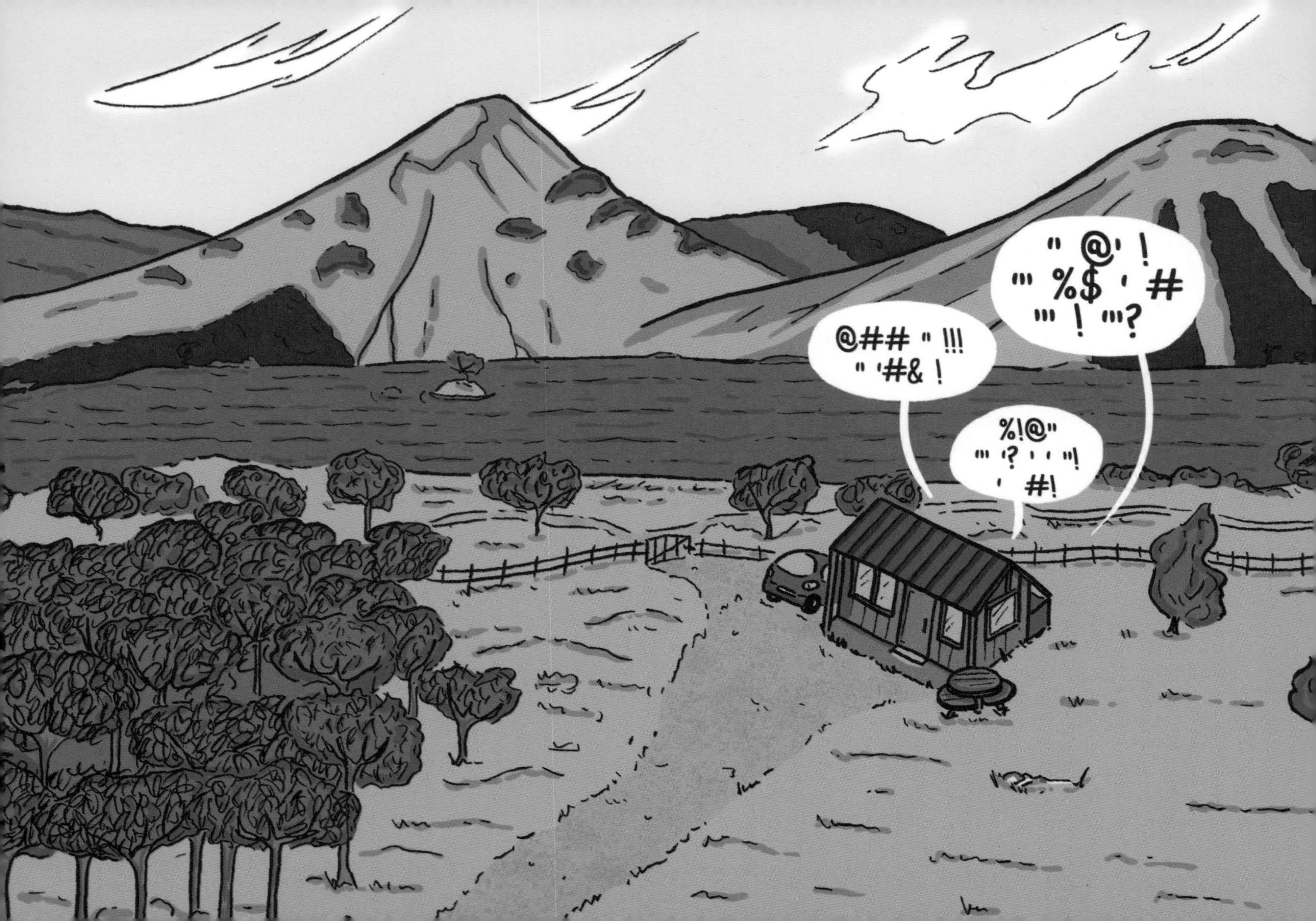

" @' ! "' %$ ' # "' ! "'?
@## " !!! " '#& !
%!@" "' '? ' ' "! ' #!

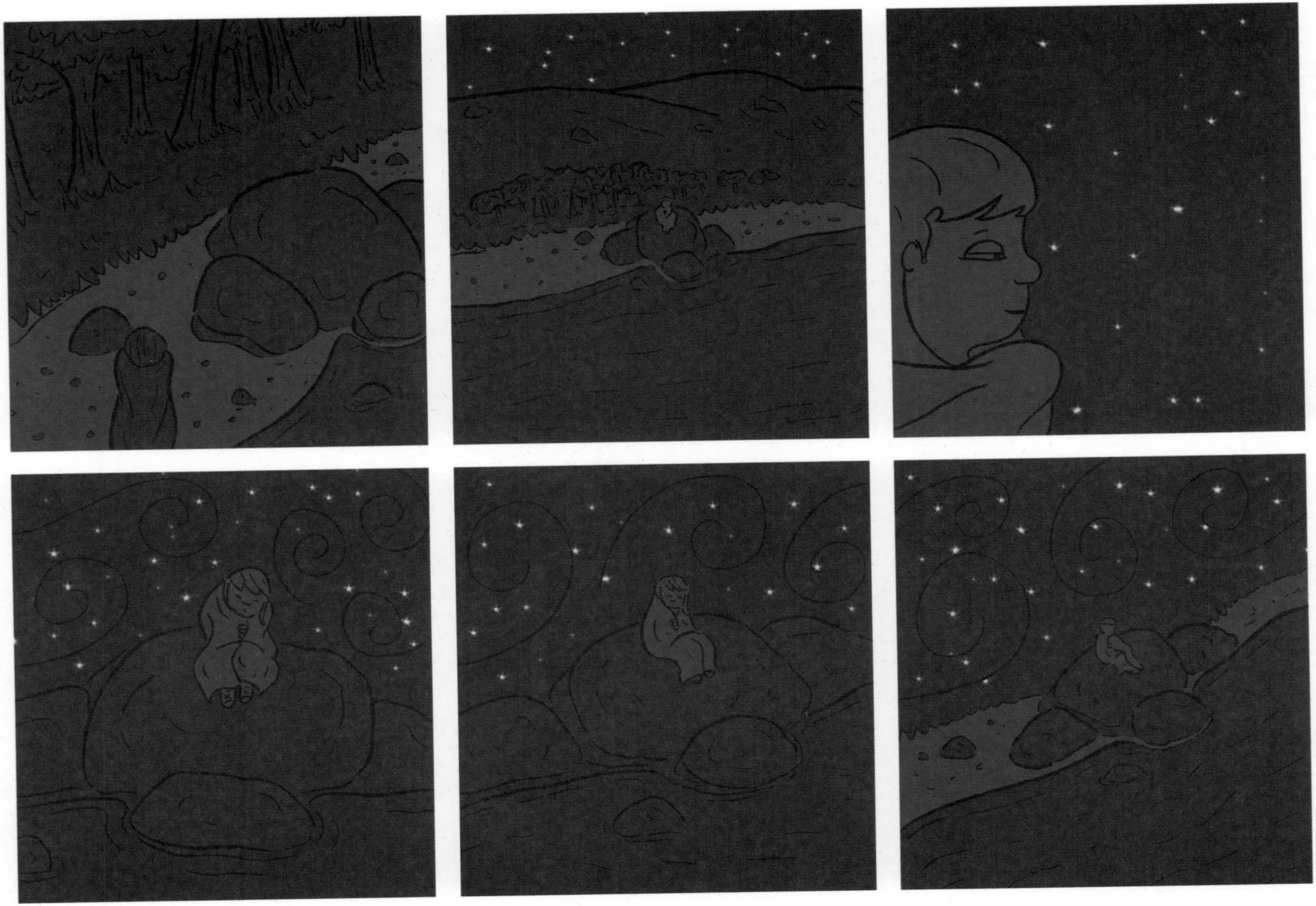

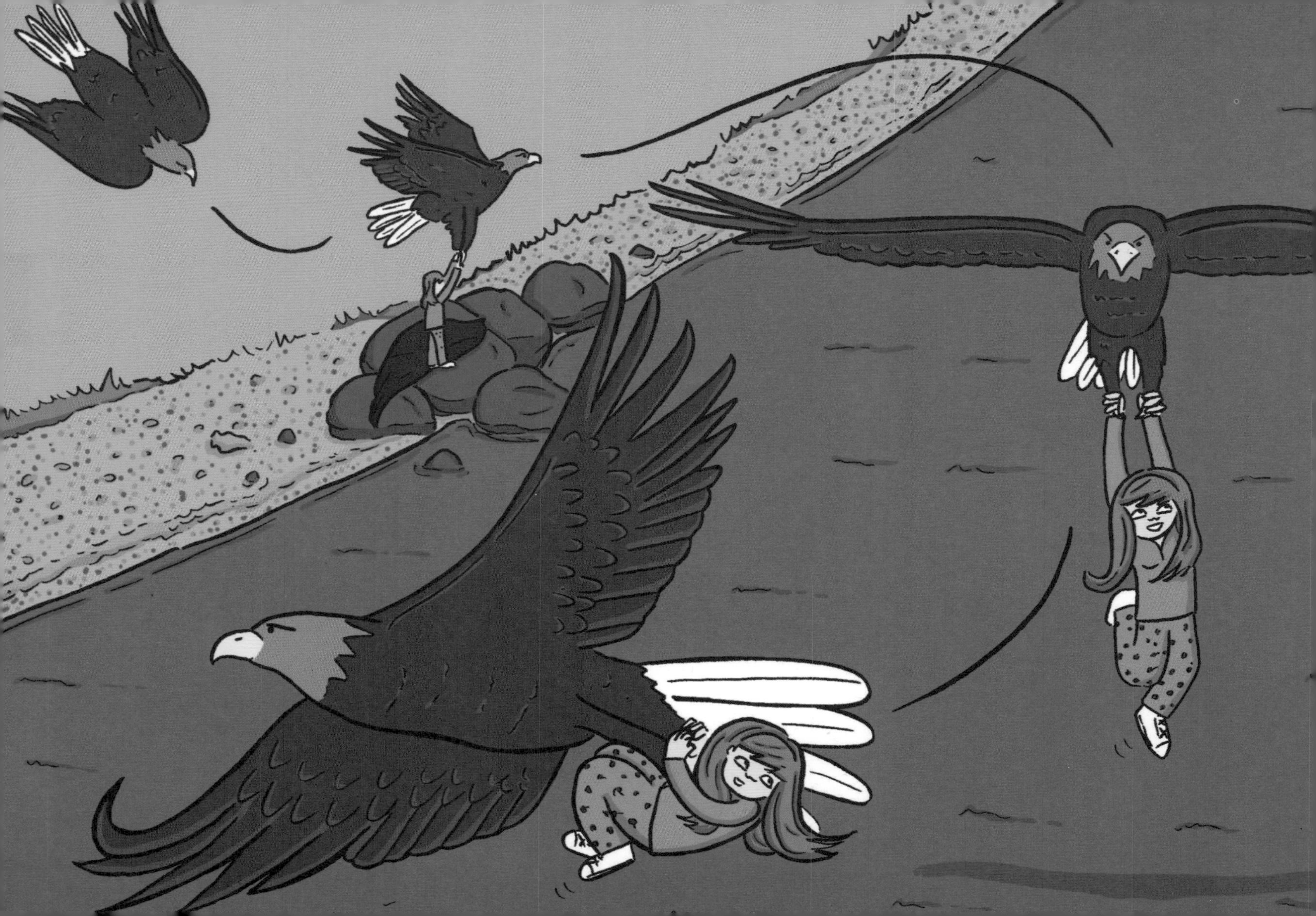

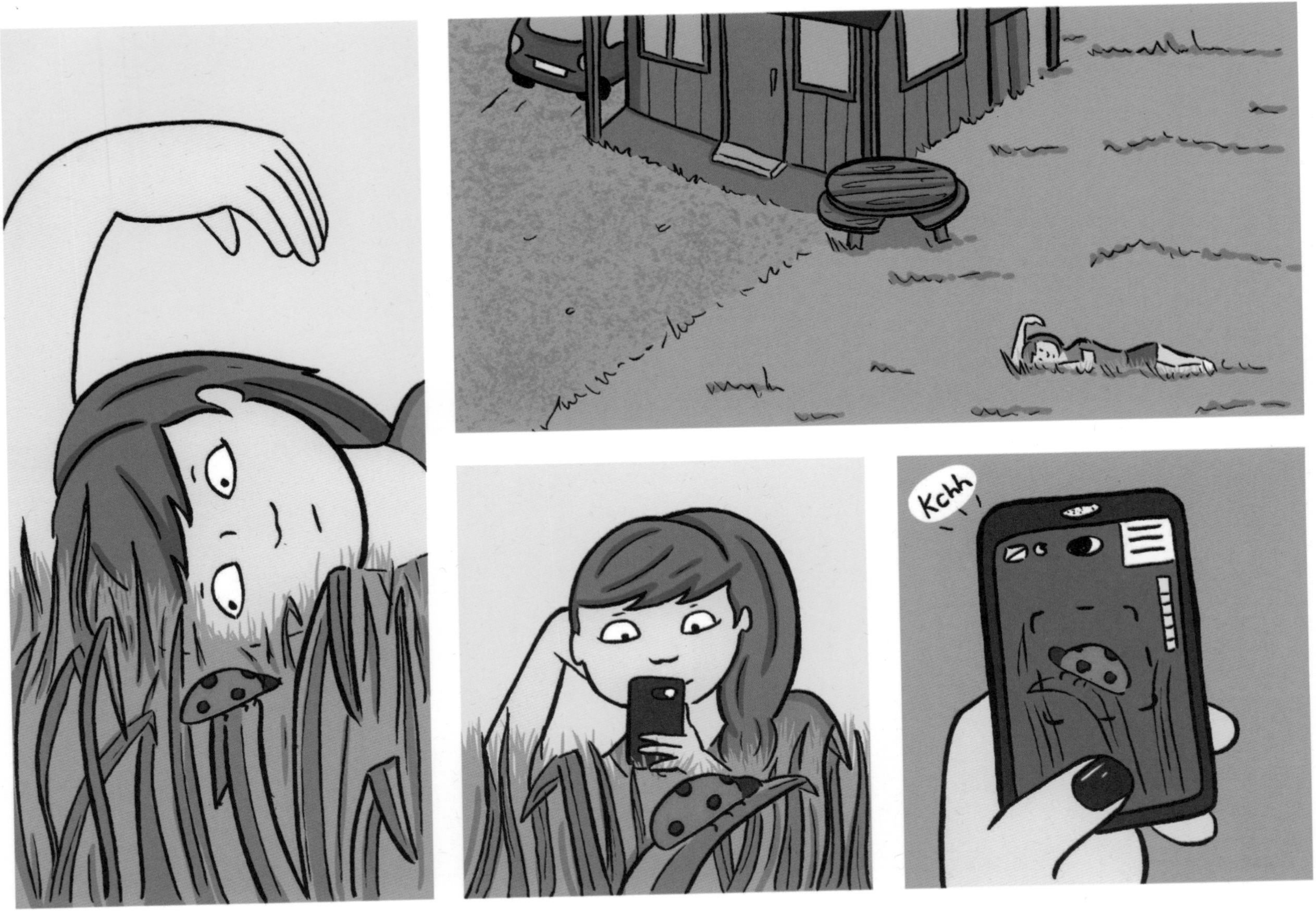
Kchh

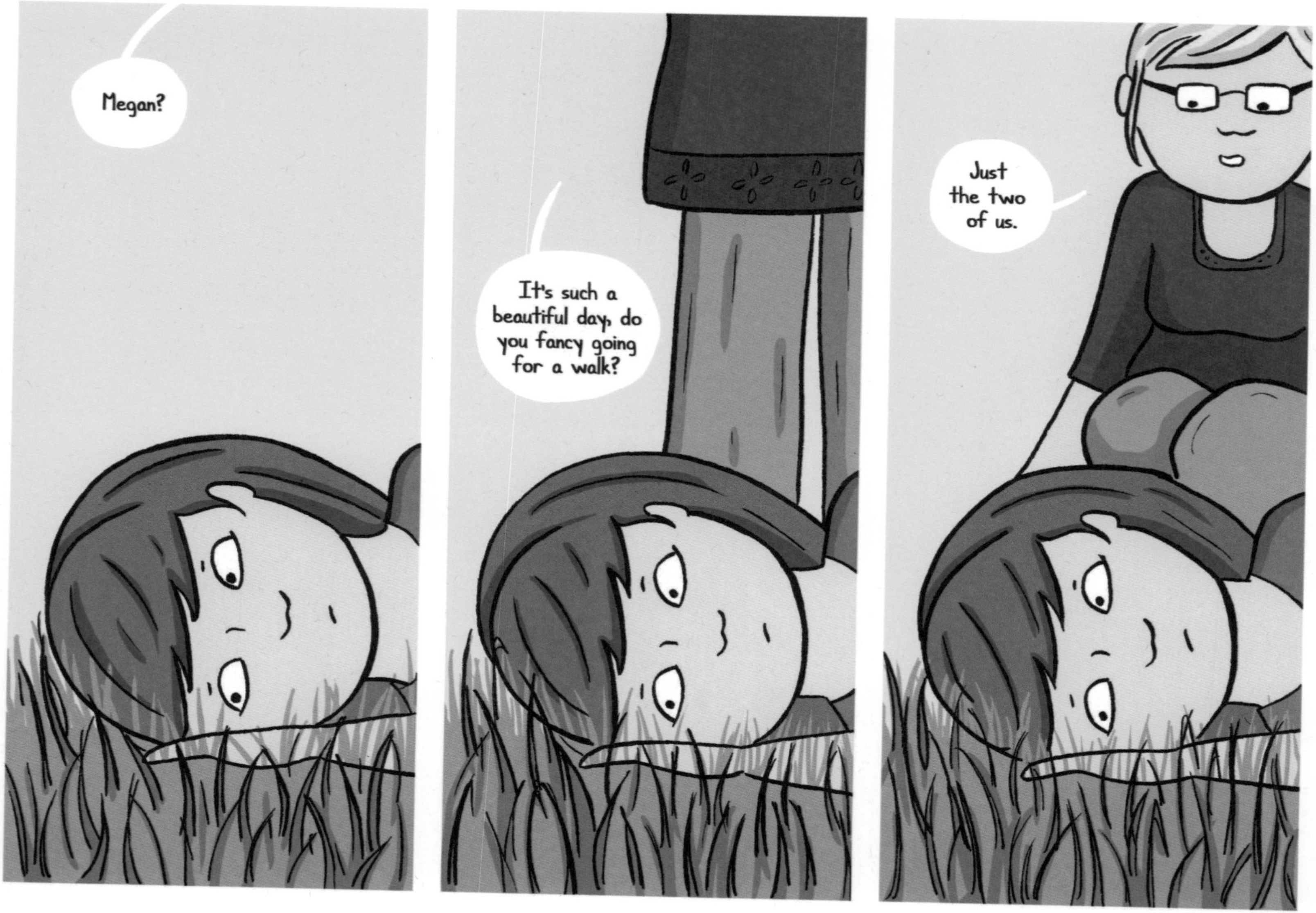
Megan?
It's such a beautiful day, do you fancy going for a walk?
Just the two of us.

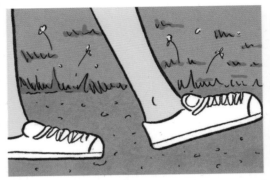

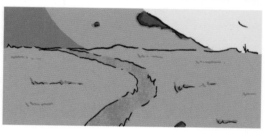

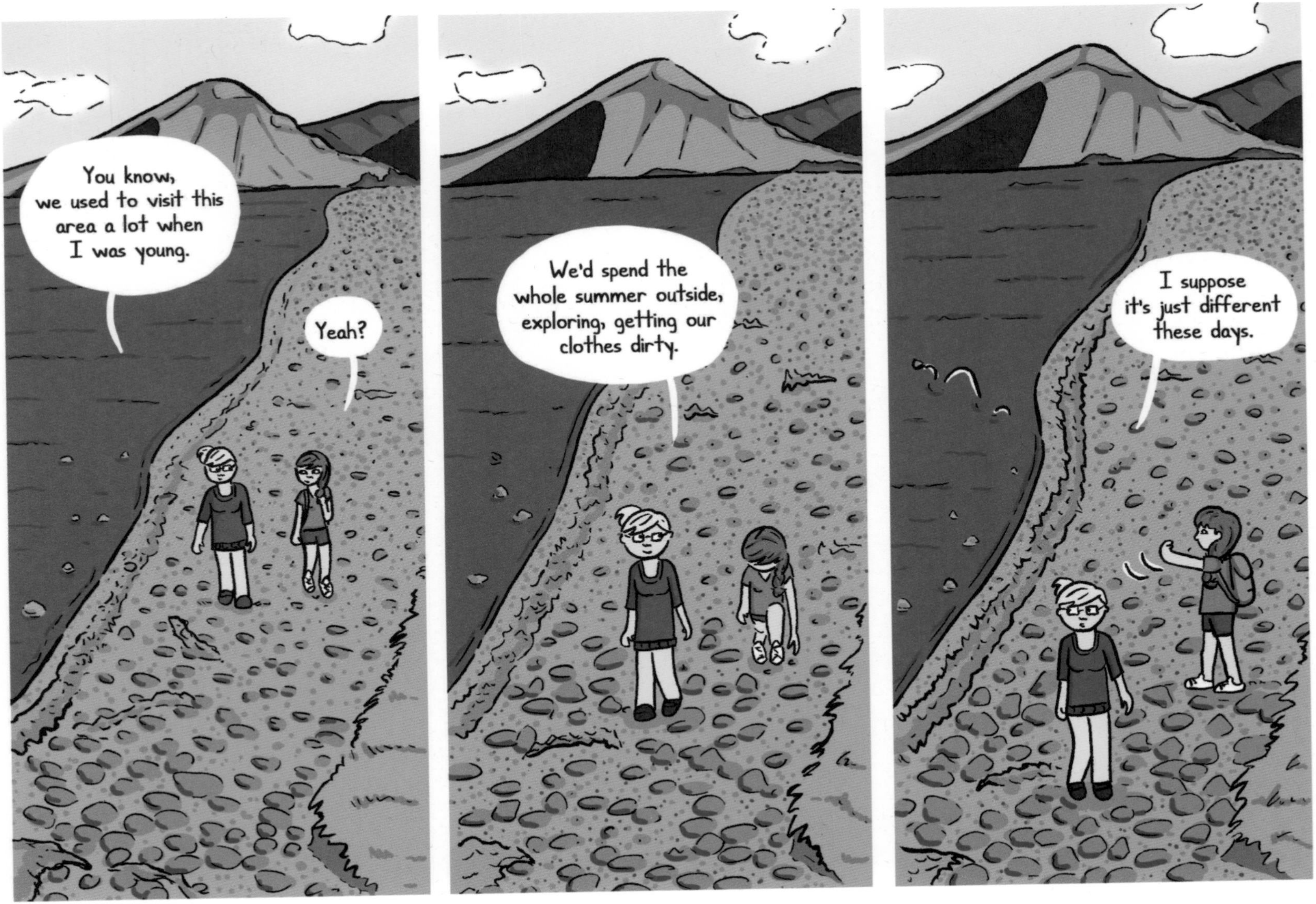
You know, we used to visit this area a lot when I was young.
Yeah?
We'd spend the whole summer outside, exploring, getting our clothes dirty.
I suppose it's just different these days.

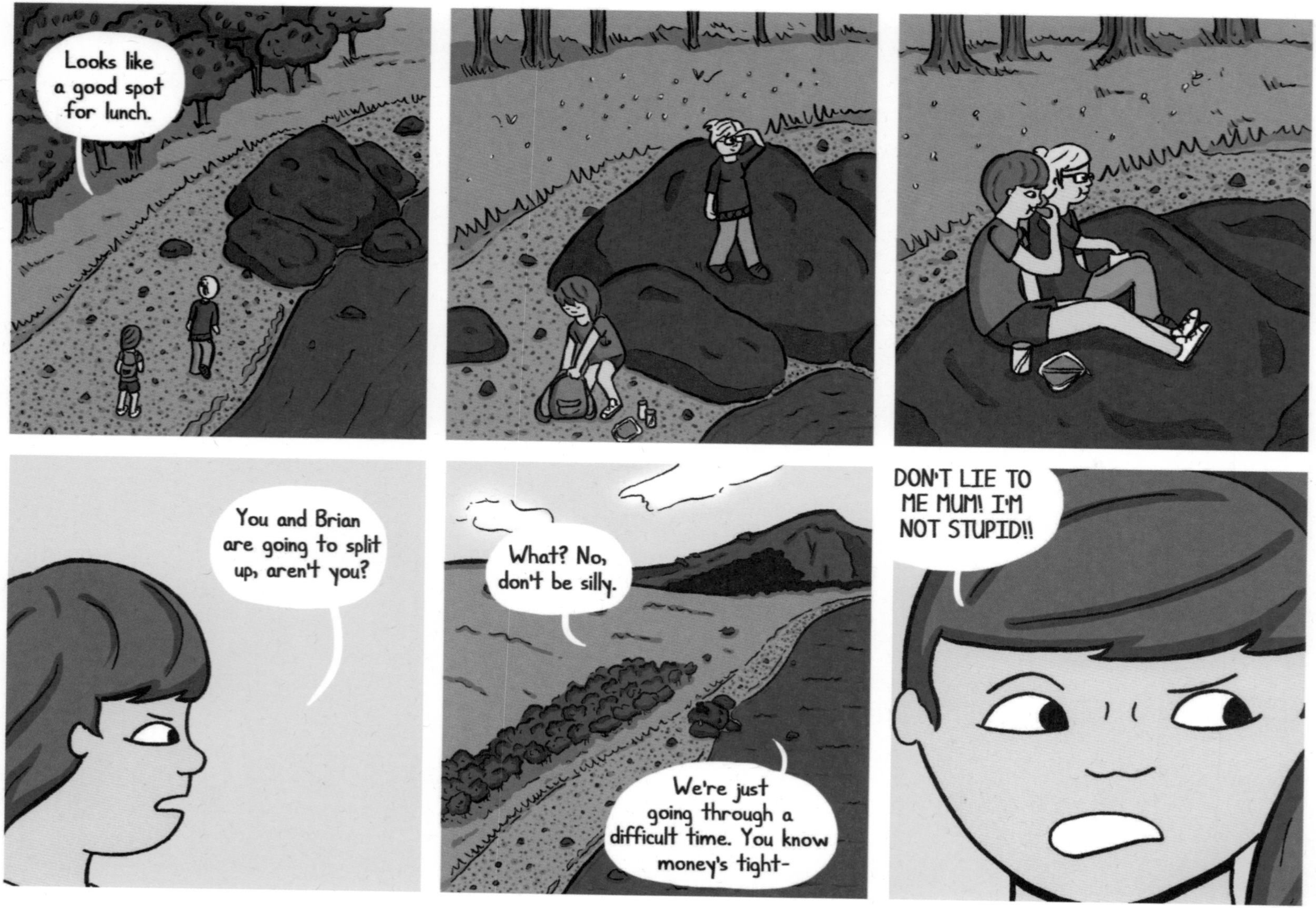
Looks like a good spot for lunch.
You and Brian are going to split up, aren't you?
What? No, don't be silly.
We're just going through a difficult time. You know money's tight-
DON'T LIE TO ME MUM! I'M NOT STUPID!!

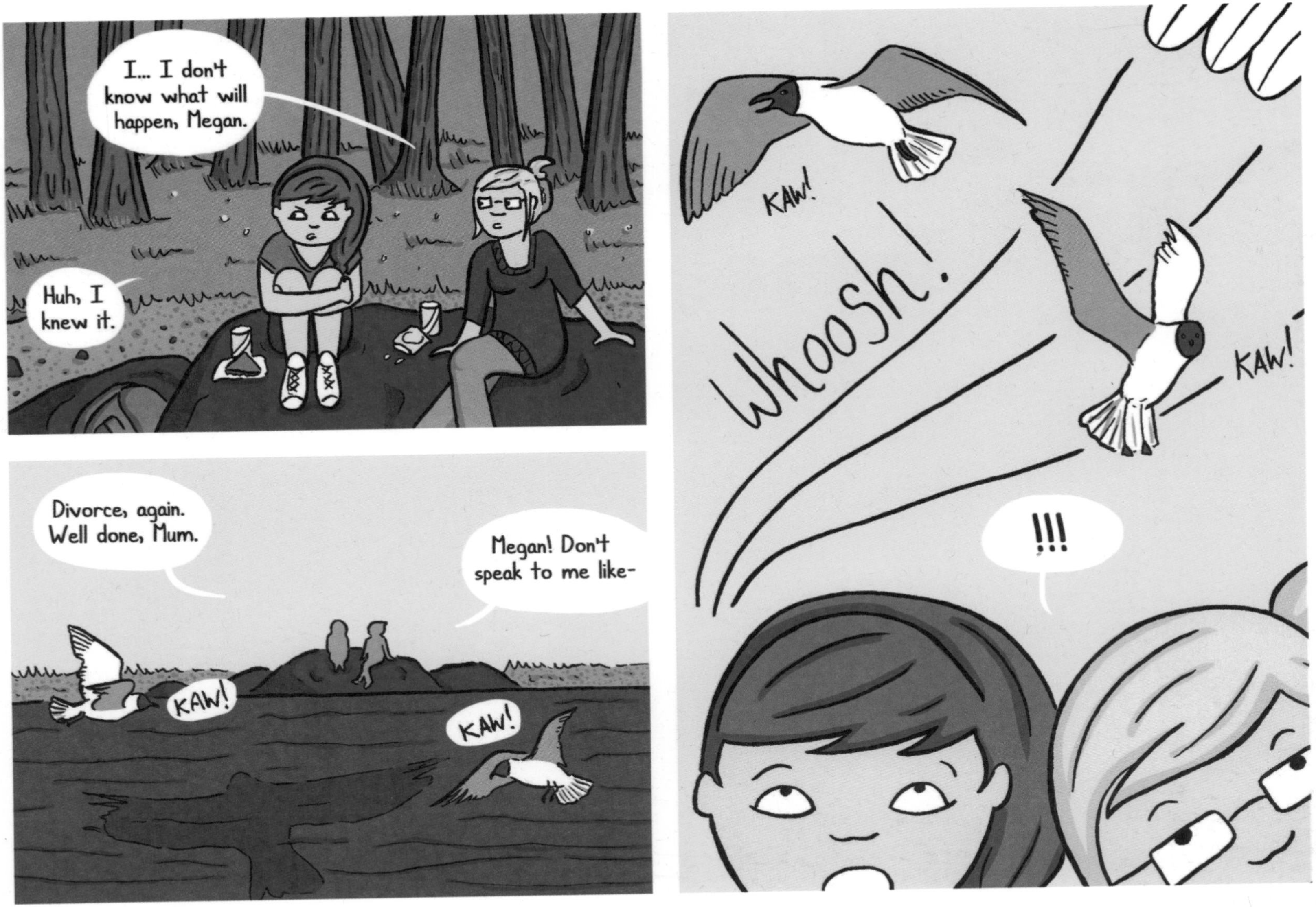
I... I don't know what will happen, Megan.
Huh, I knew it.
Divorce, again. Well done, Mum.
Megan! Don't speak to me like-
KAW!
KAW!
KAW!
Whoosh!
KAW!
!!!

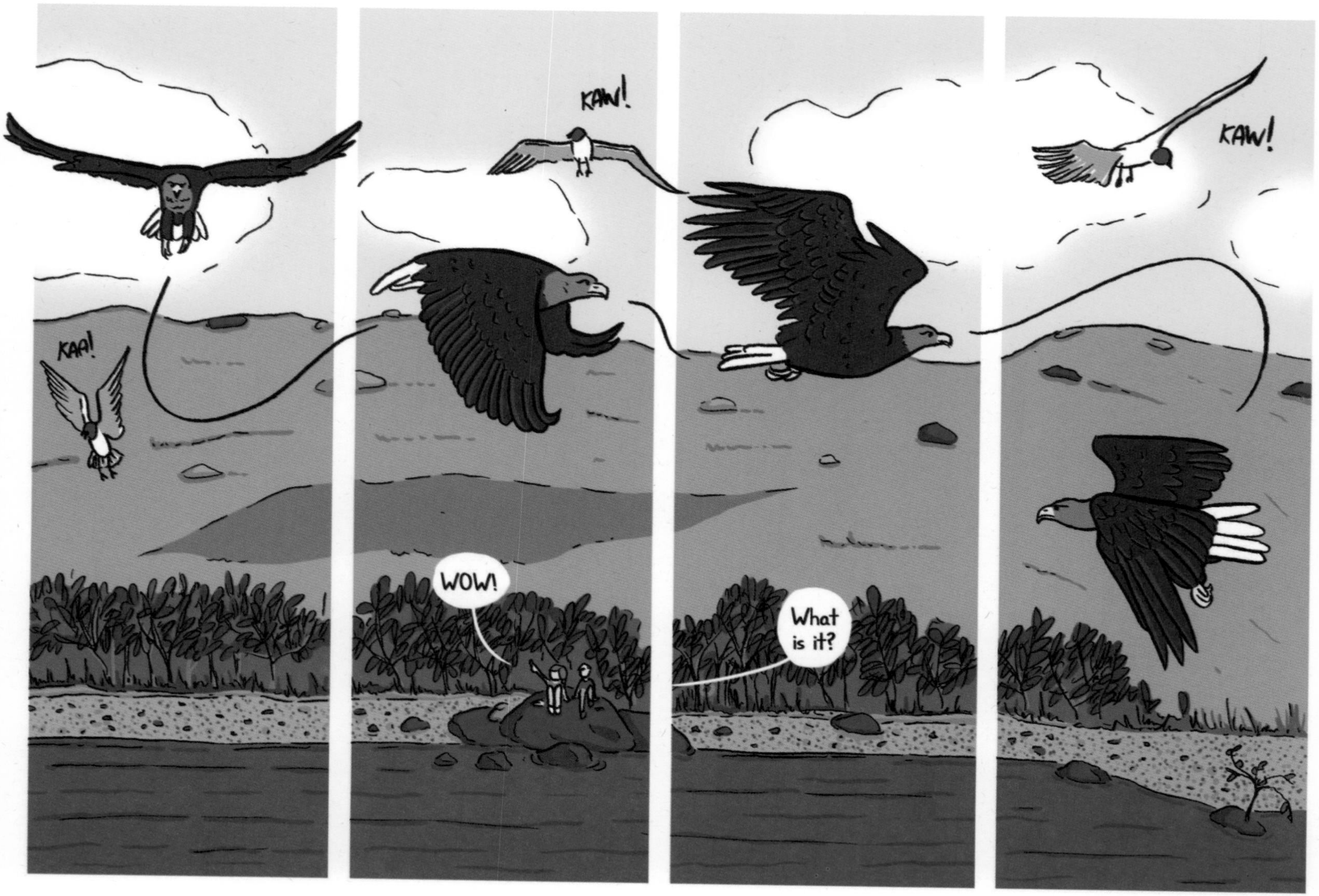
KAA!
KAW!
WOW!
What is it?
KAW!

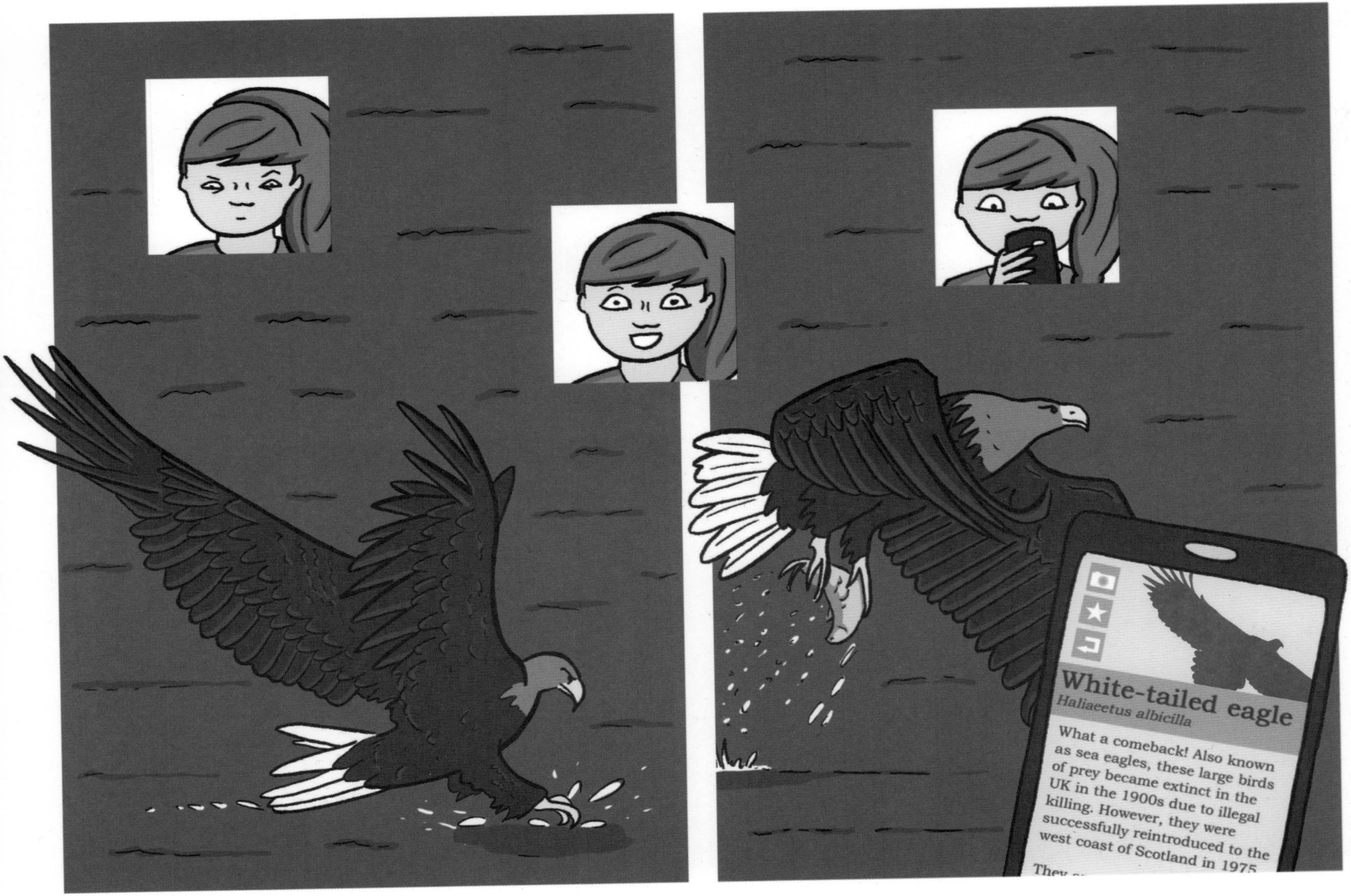
White-tailed eagle
Haliaeetus albicilla
What a comeback! Also known as sea eagles, these large birds of prey became extinct in the UK in the 1900s due to illegal killing. However, they were successfully reintroduced to the west coast of Scotland in 1975.

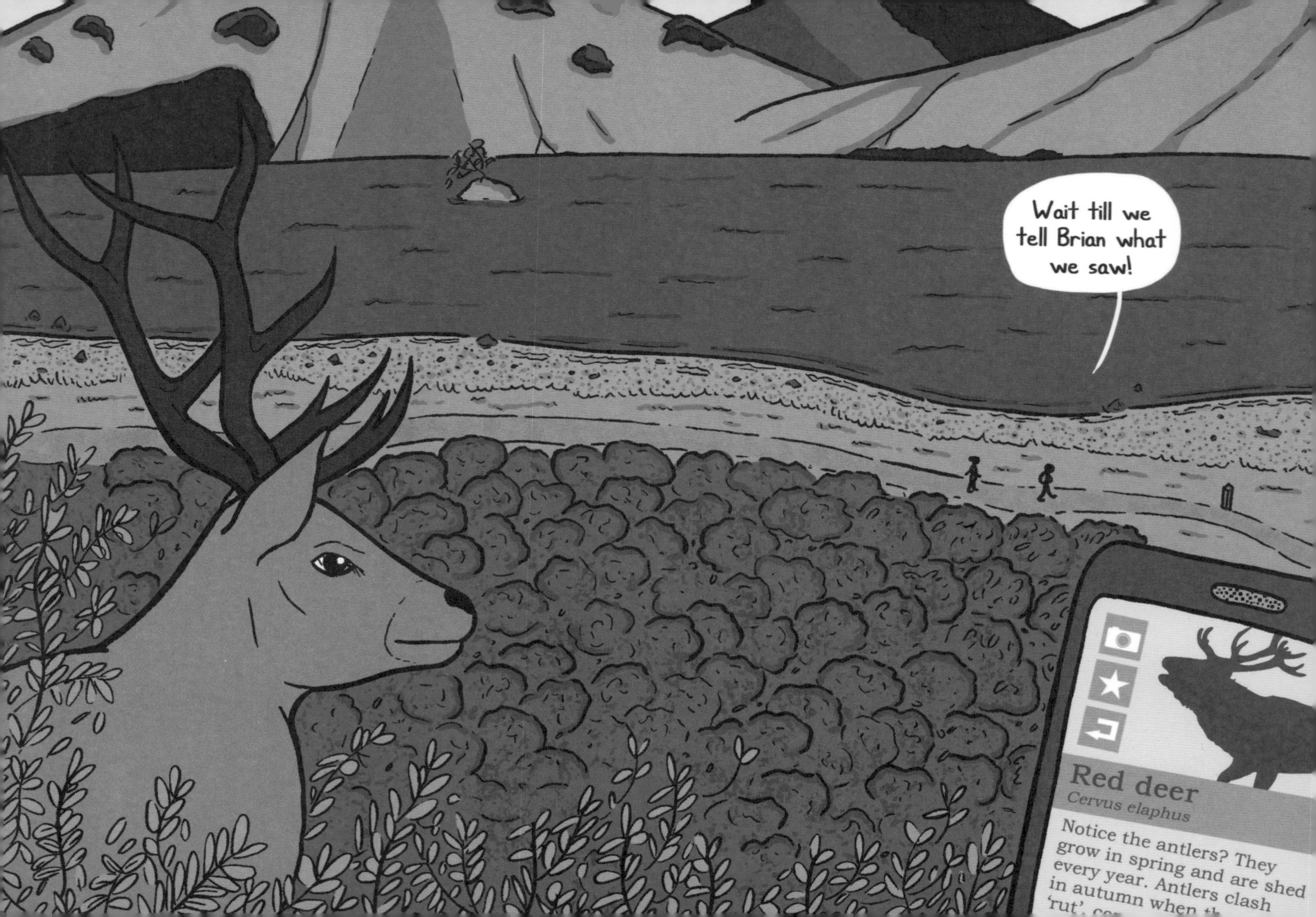
Wait till we tell Brian what we saw!
Red deer
Cervus elaphus
Notice the antlers? They grow in spring and are shed every year. Antlers clash in autumn when

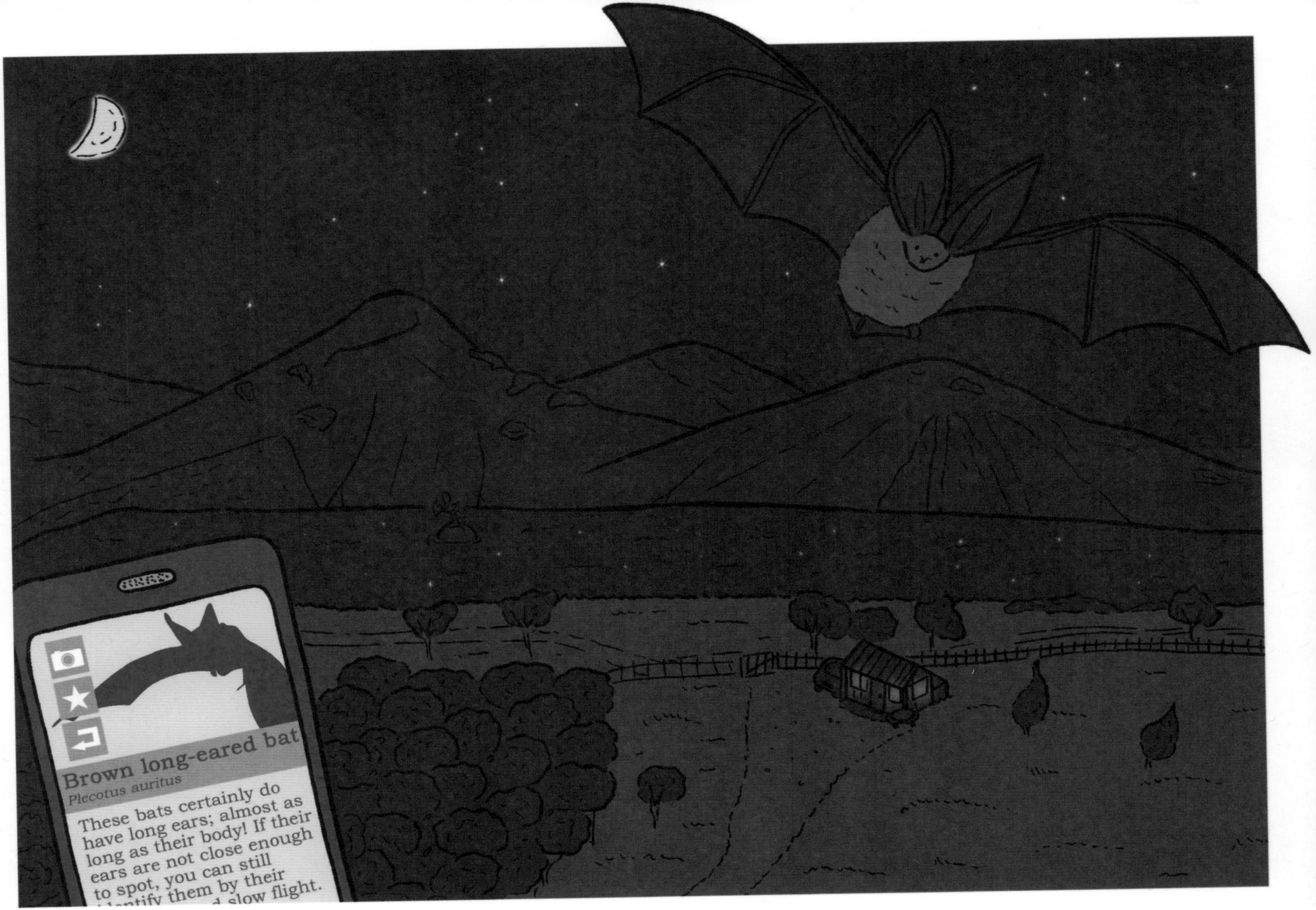
Brown long-eared bat
Plecotus auritus
These bats certainly do
have long ears; almost as
long as their body! If their
ears are not close enough
to spot, you can still
them by their
slow flight.

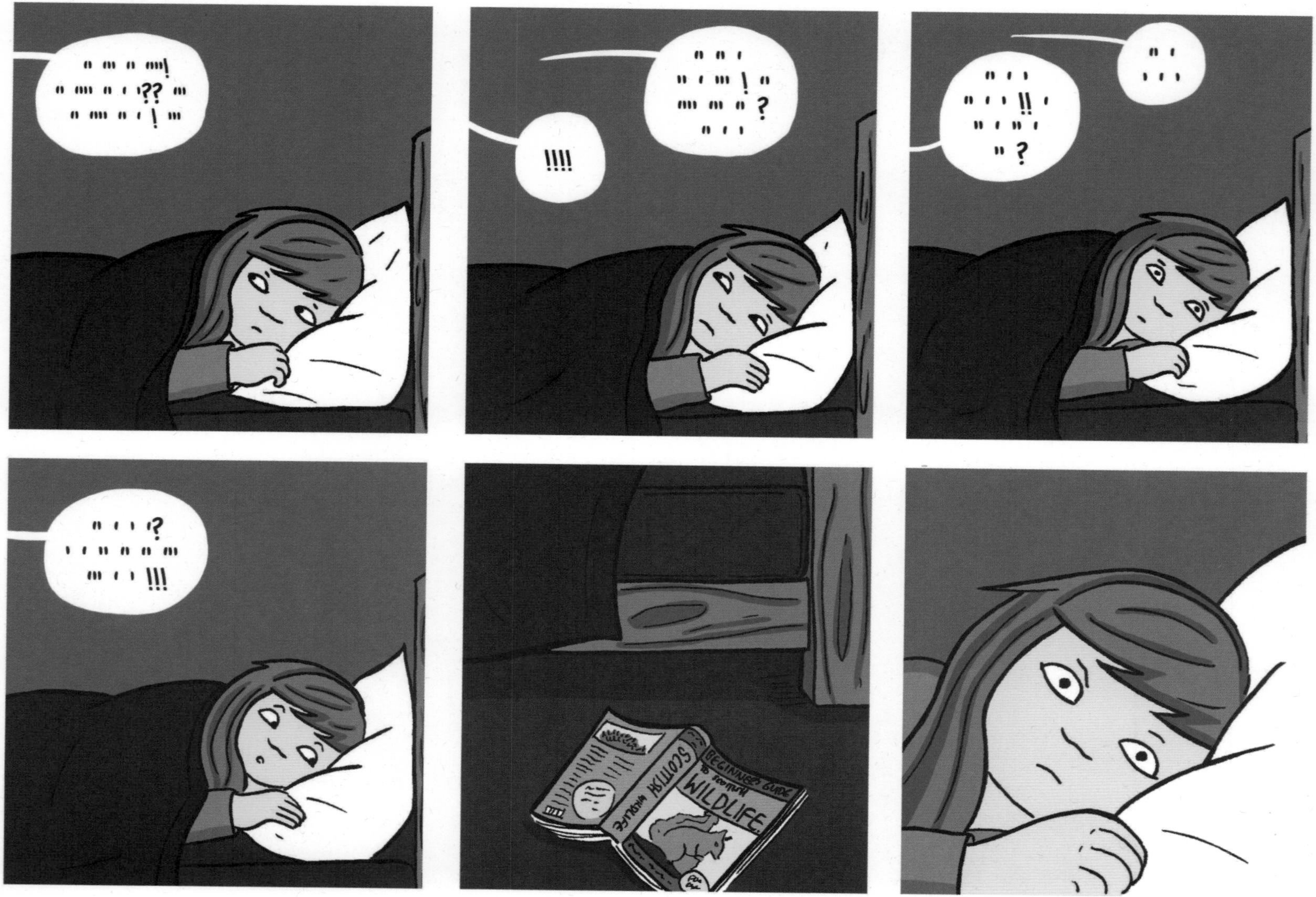
!!!!
BEGINNERS GUIDE
WILDLIFE

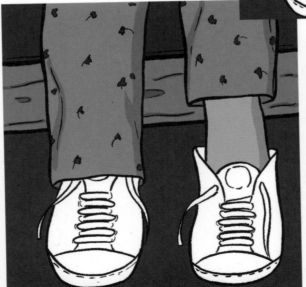

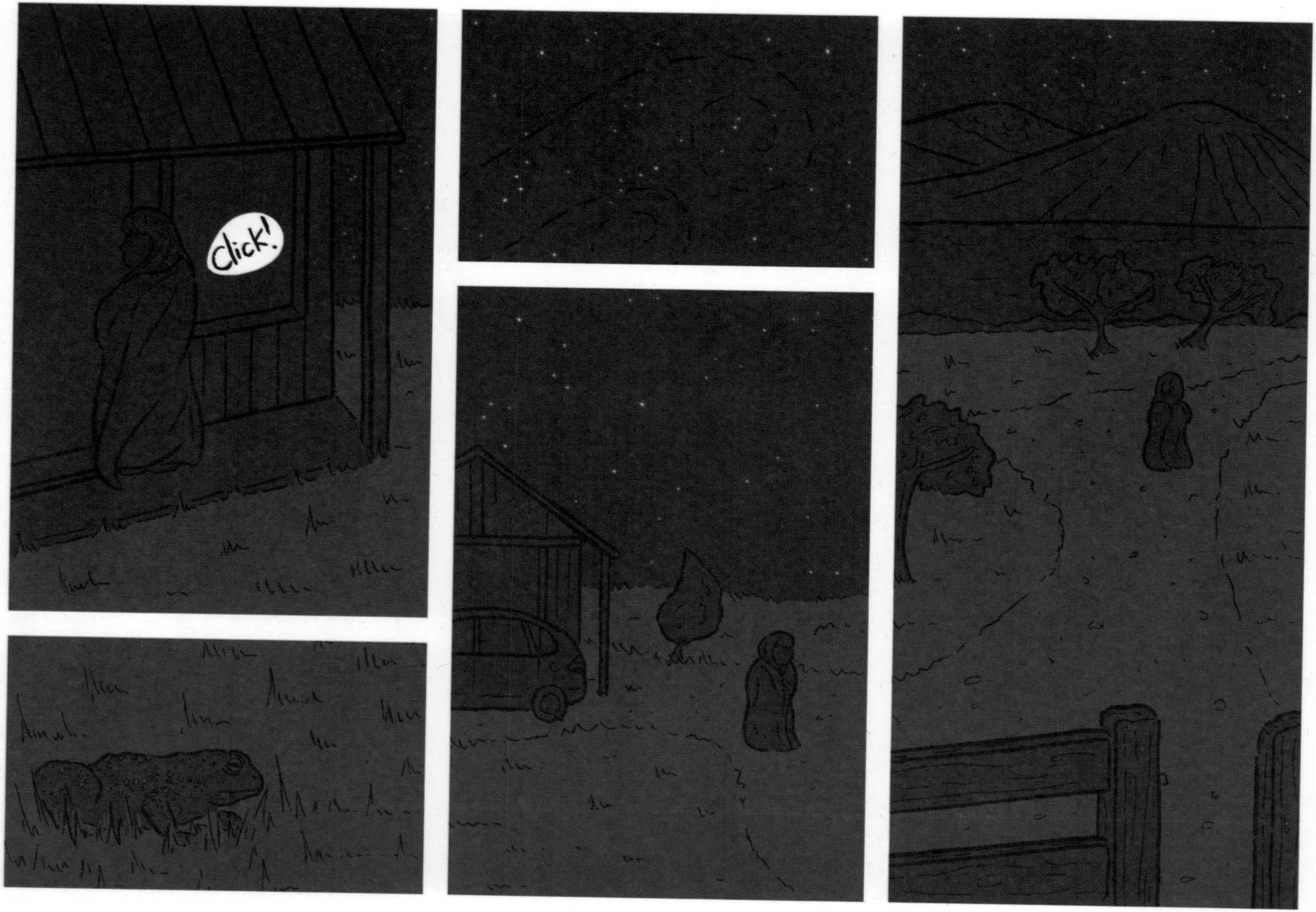
Click!

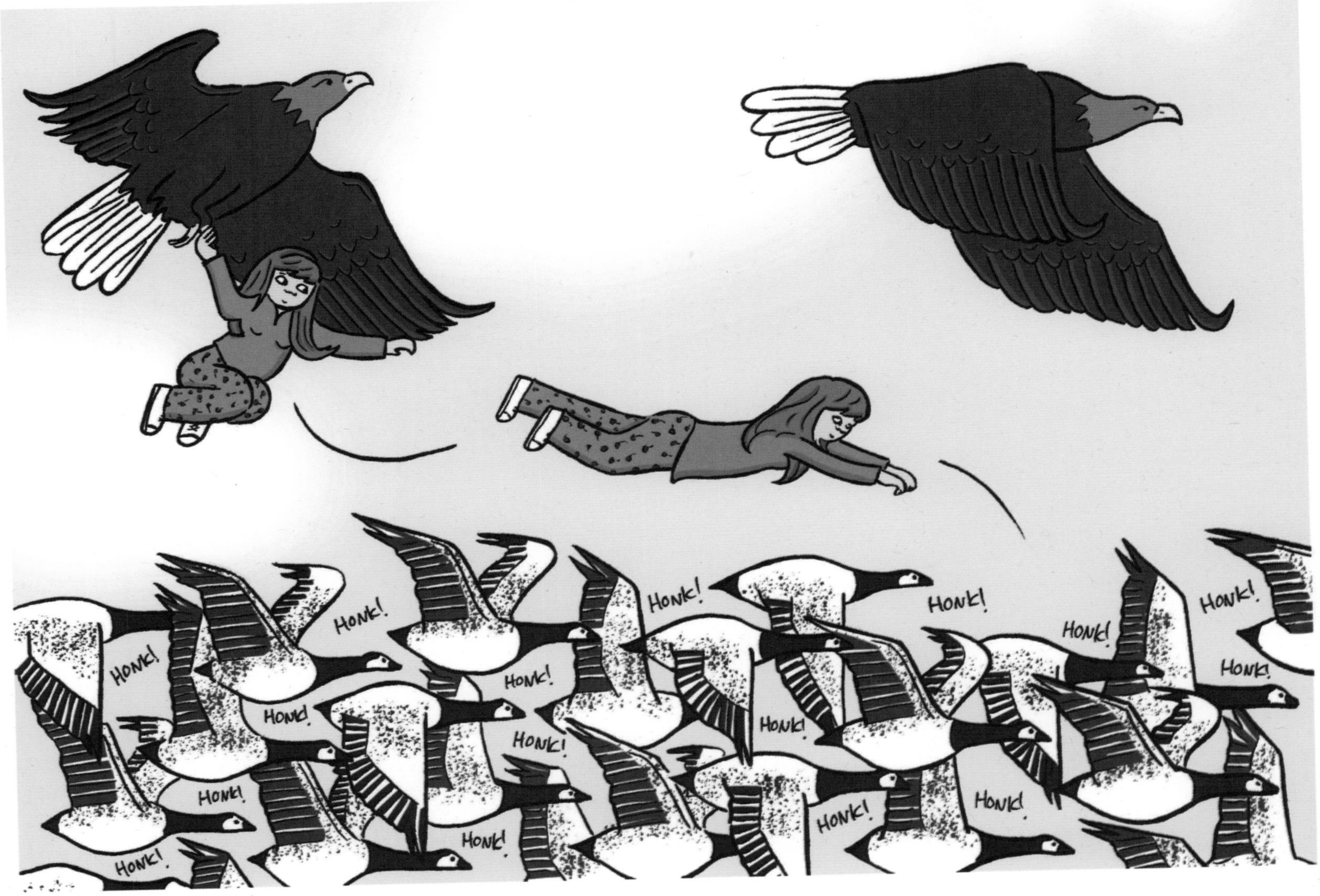
HONK!
HONK!
HONK!
HONK!
HONK!
HONK!
HONK!
HONK!
HONK!
HONK!
HONK!
HONK!
HONK!
HONK!
HONK!
HONK!

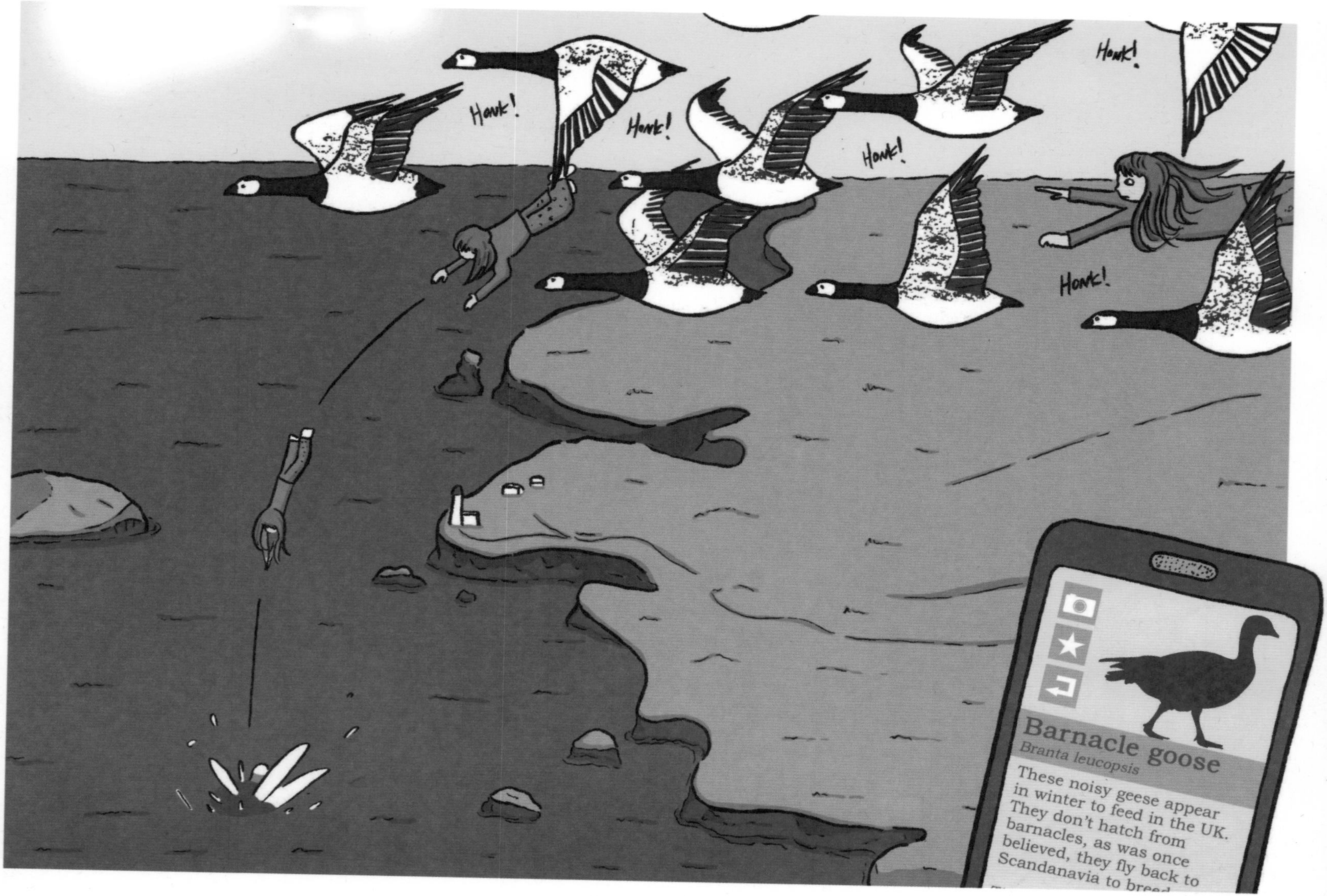
HONK!
HONK!
HONK!
HONK!
HONK!
Barnacle goose
Branta leucopsis
These noisy geese appear in winter to feed in the UK. They don't hatch from barnacles, as was once believed, they fly back to Scandanavia to breed

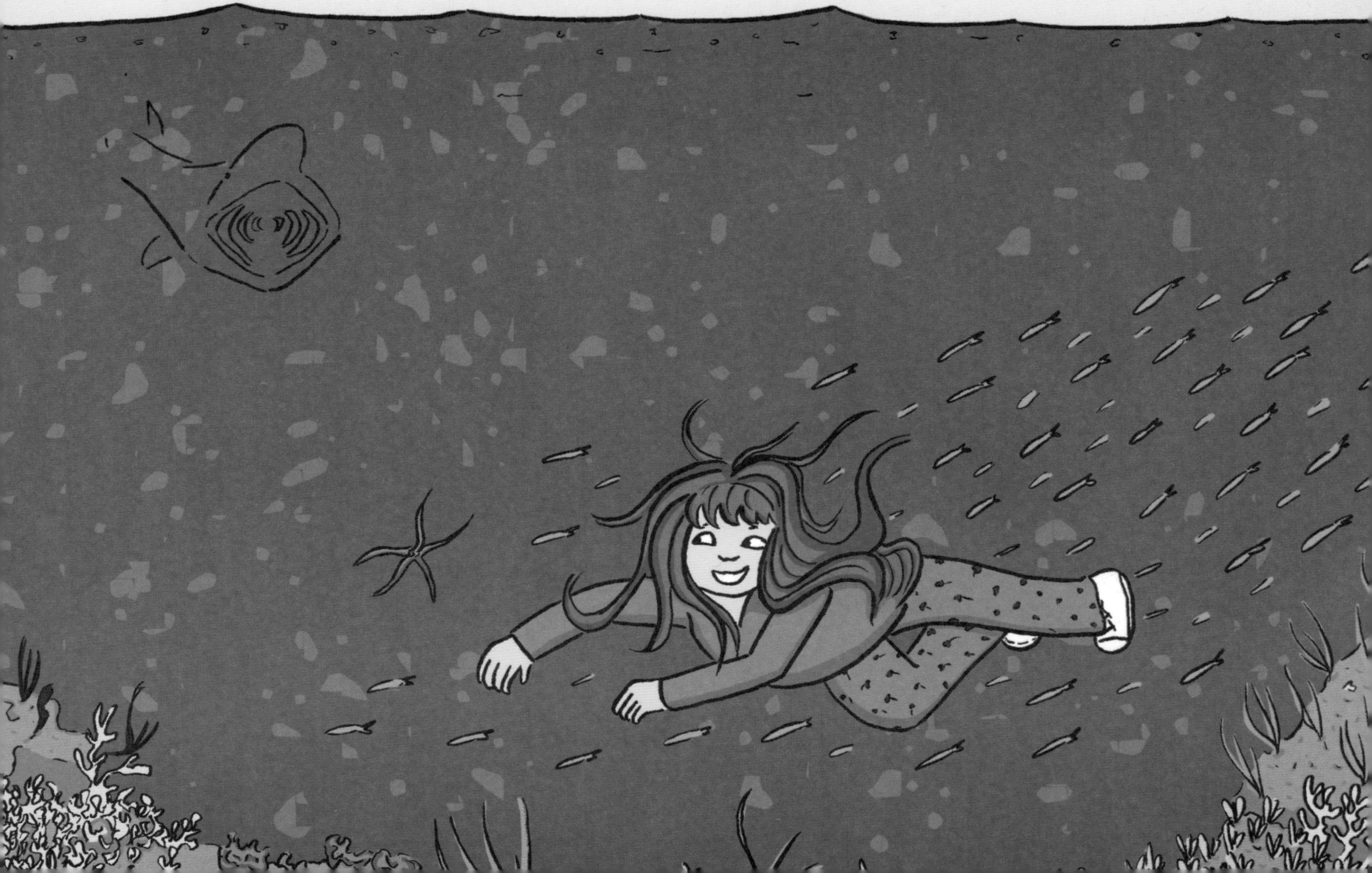

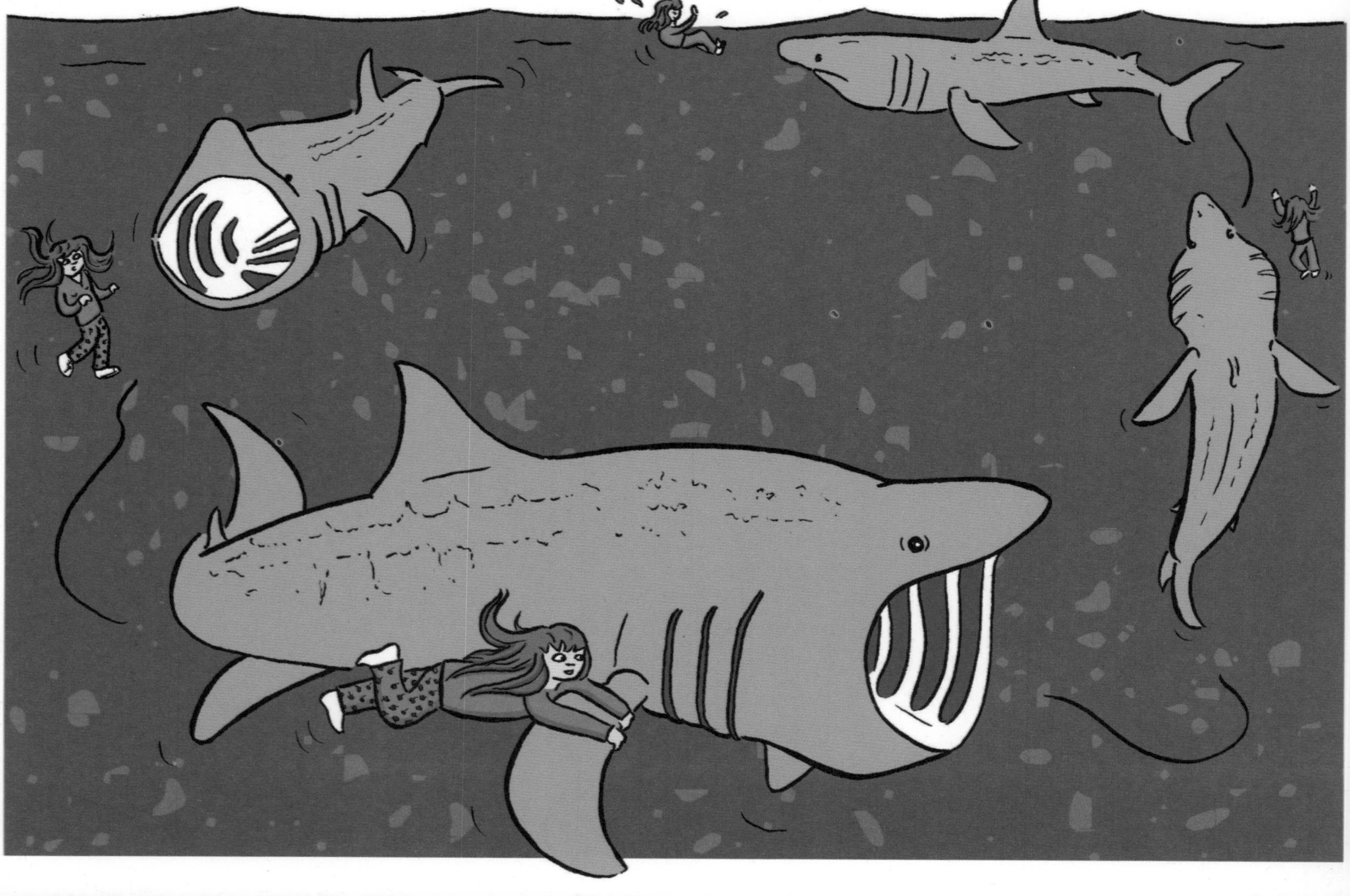

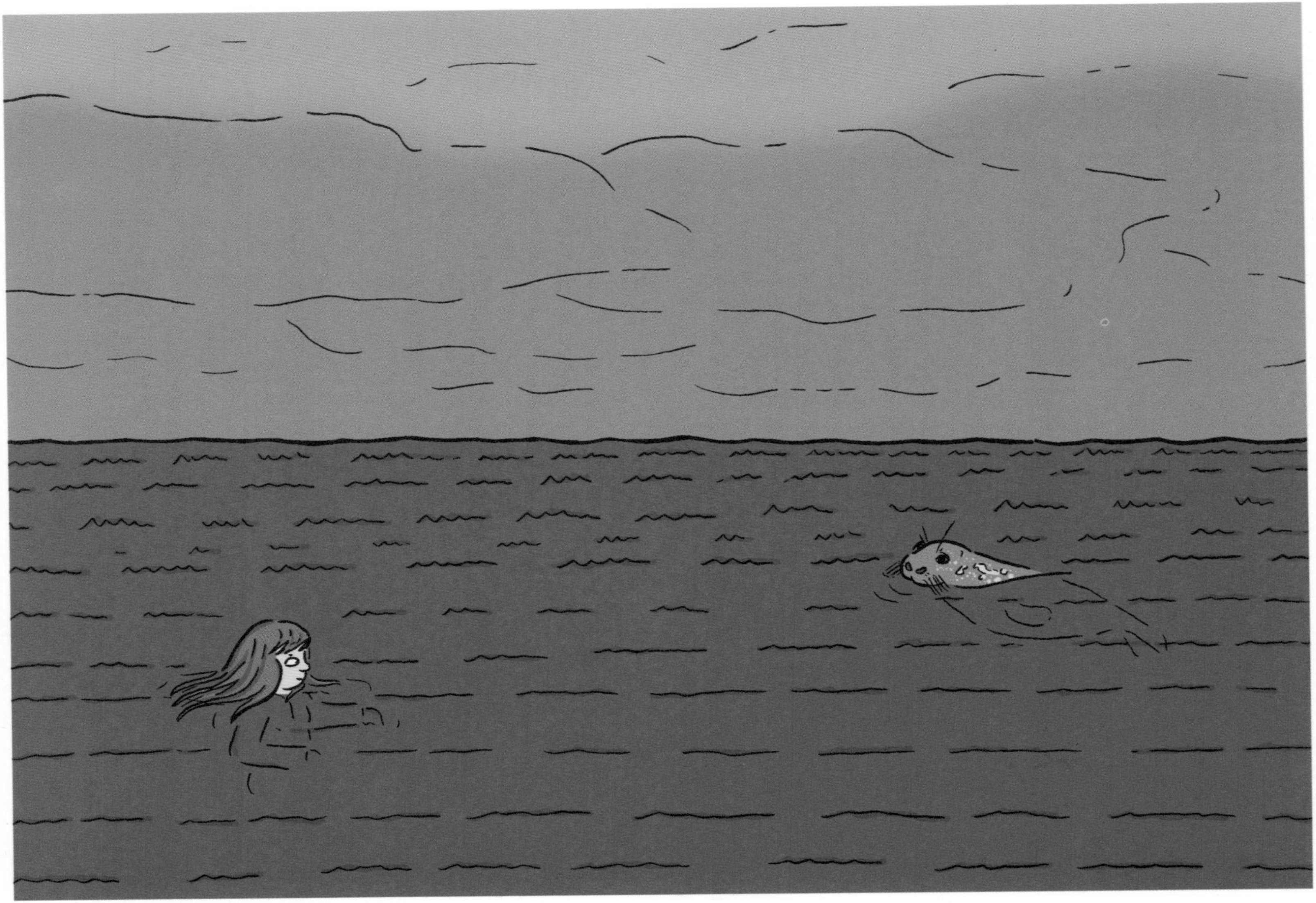

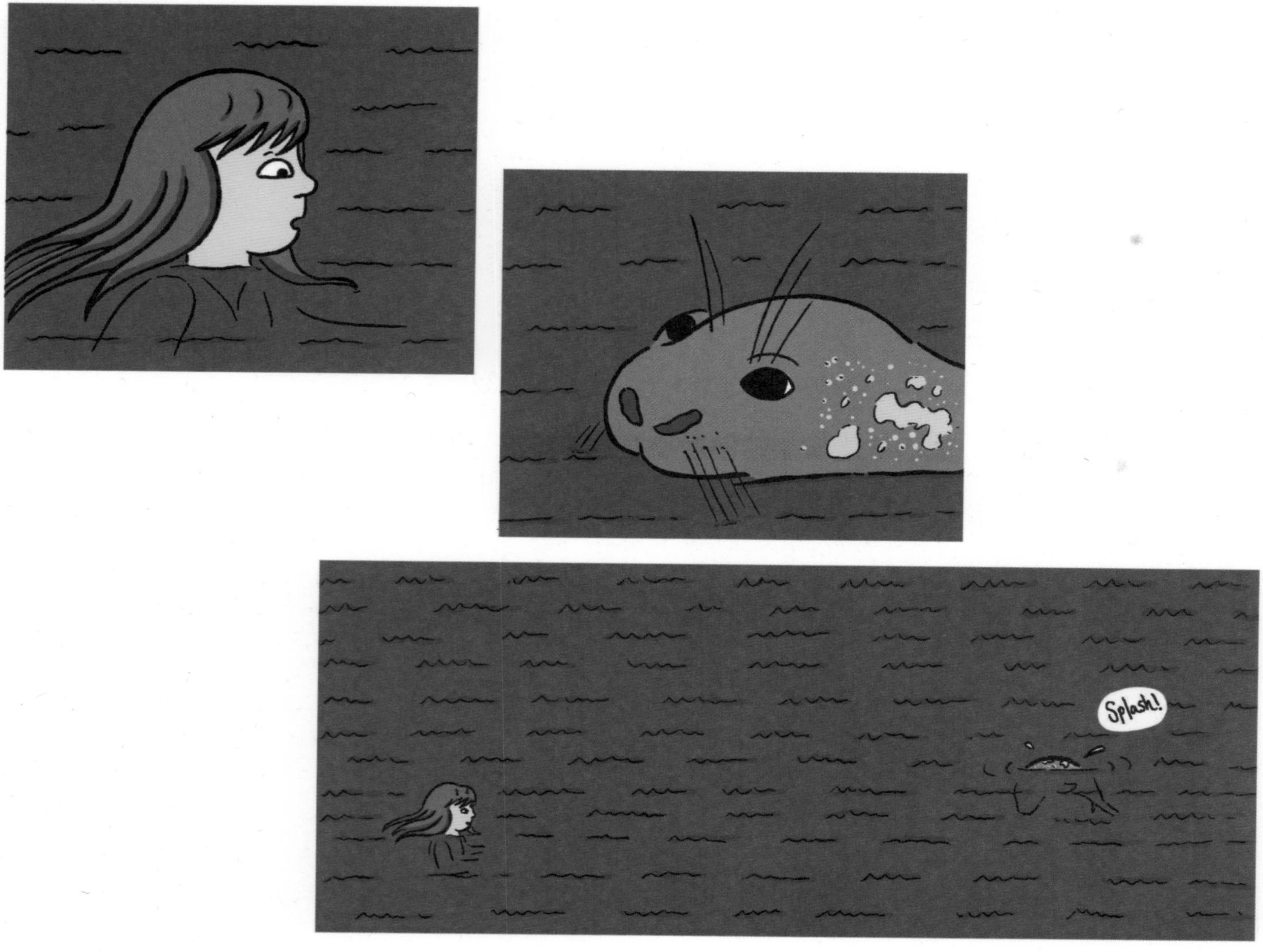
Splash!

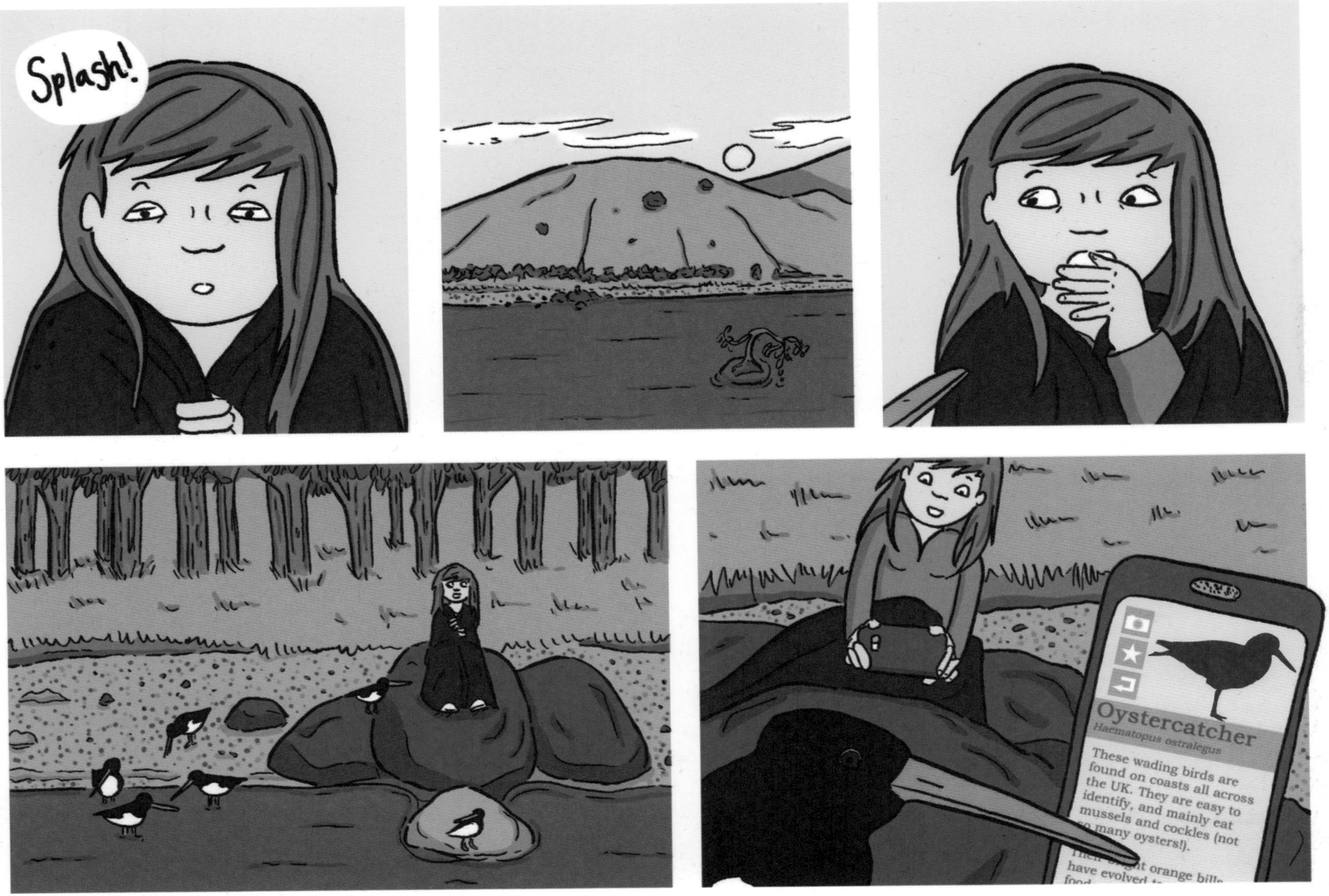
Splash!
Oystercatcher
Haematopus ostralegus
These wading birds are found on coasts all across the UK. They are easy to identify, and mainly eat mussels and cockles (not many oysters!).
orange bills
have evolved

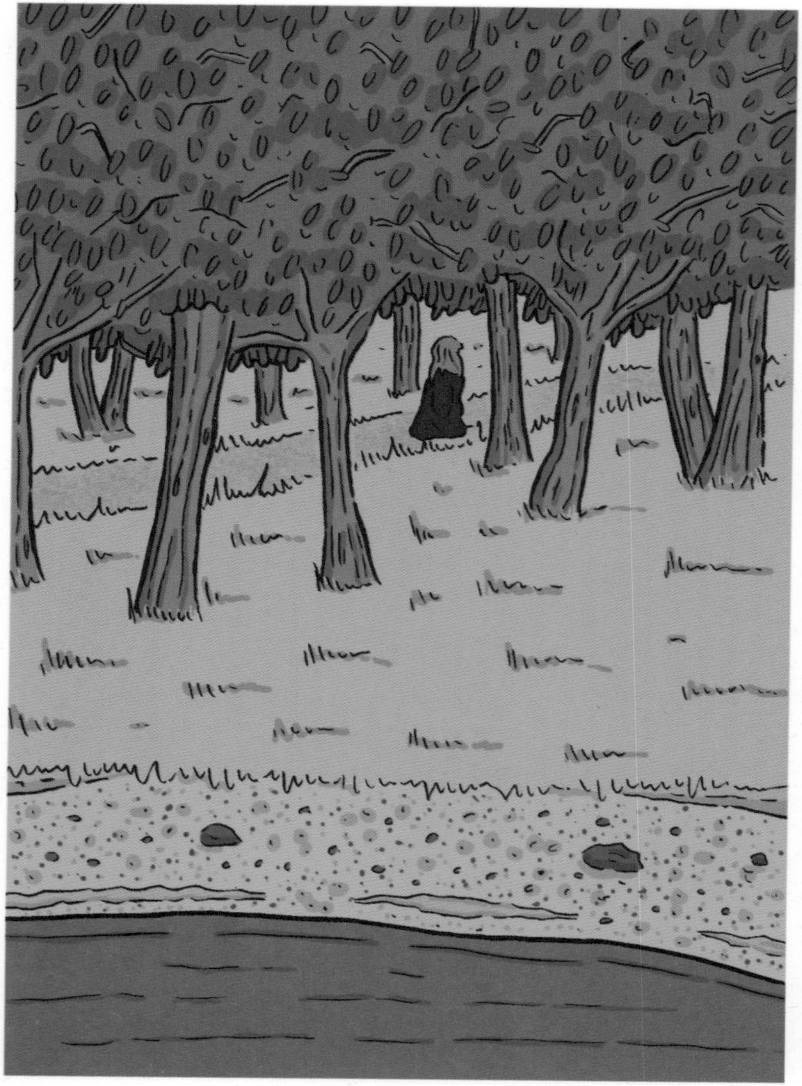
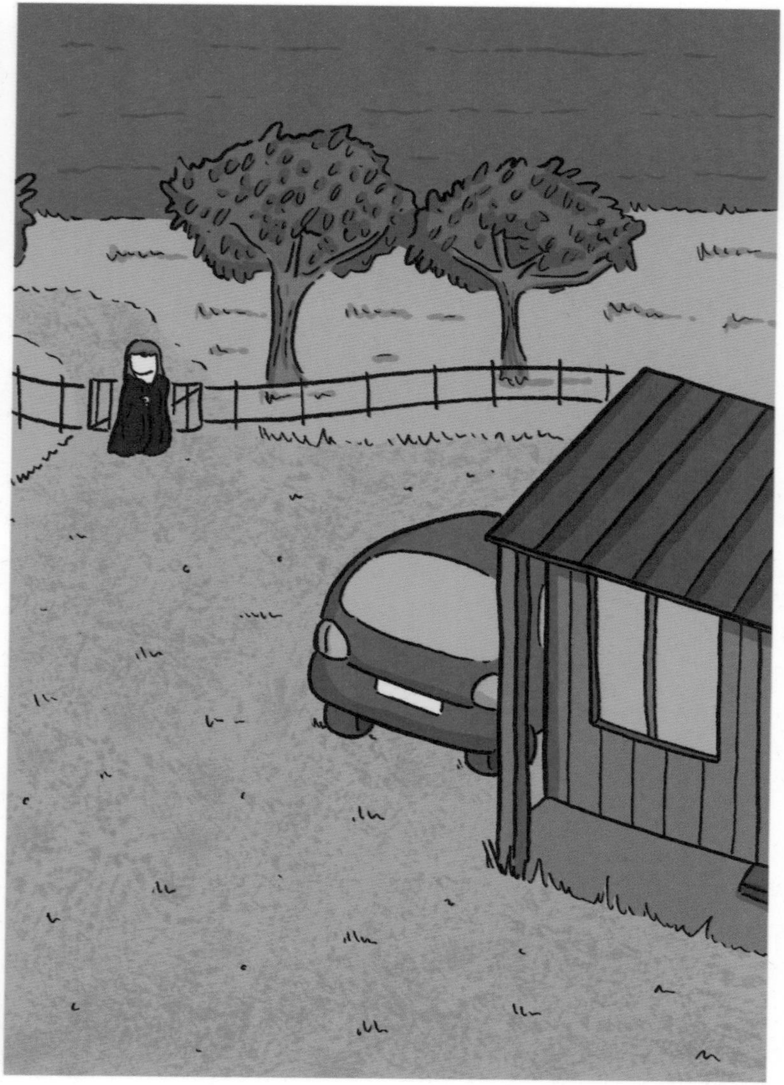

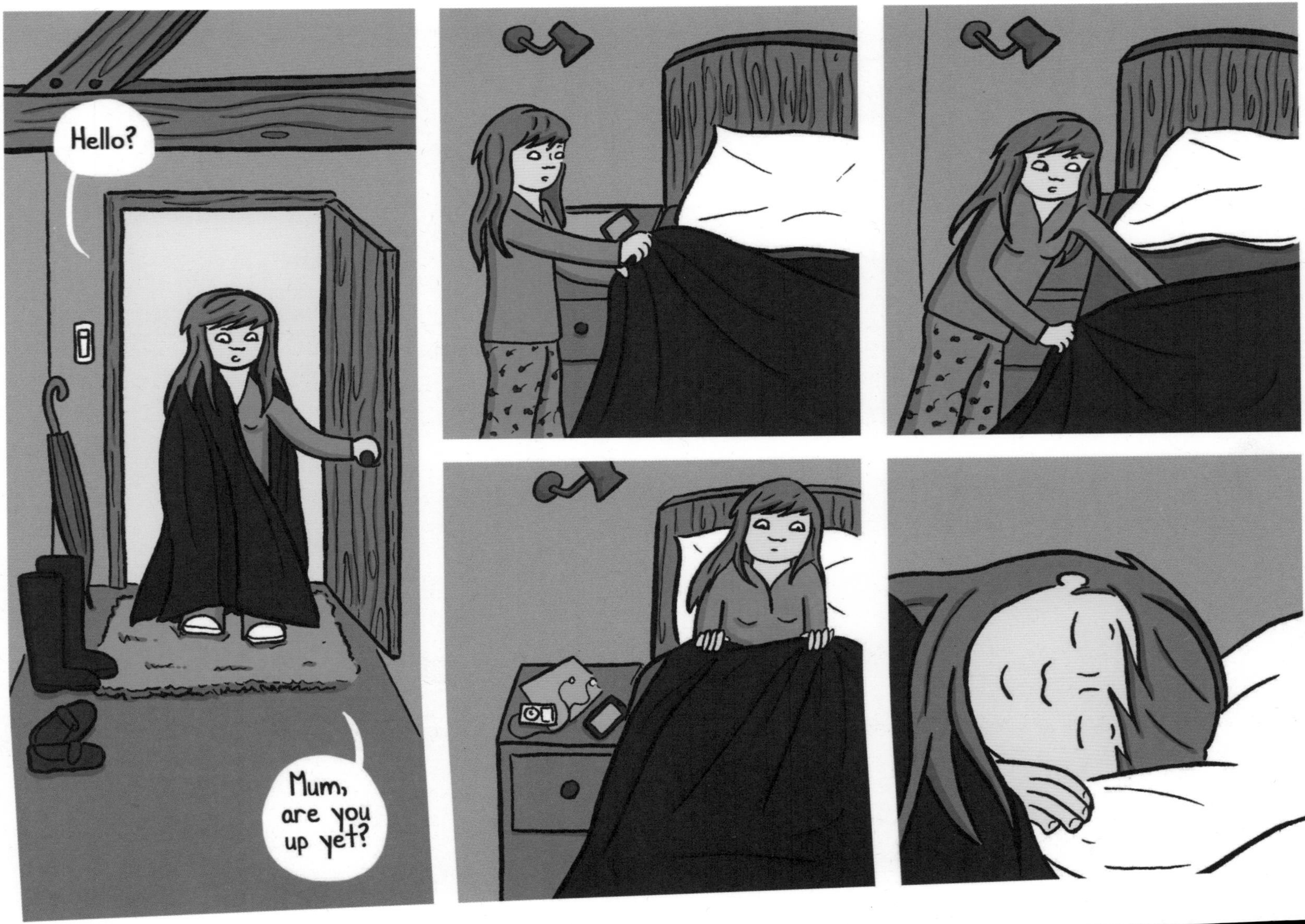
Hello?
Mum, are you up yet?

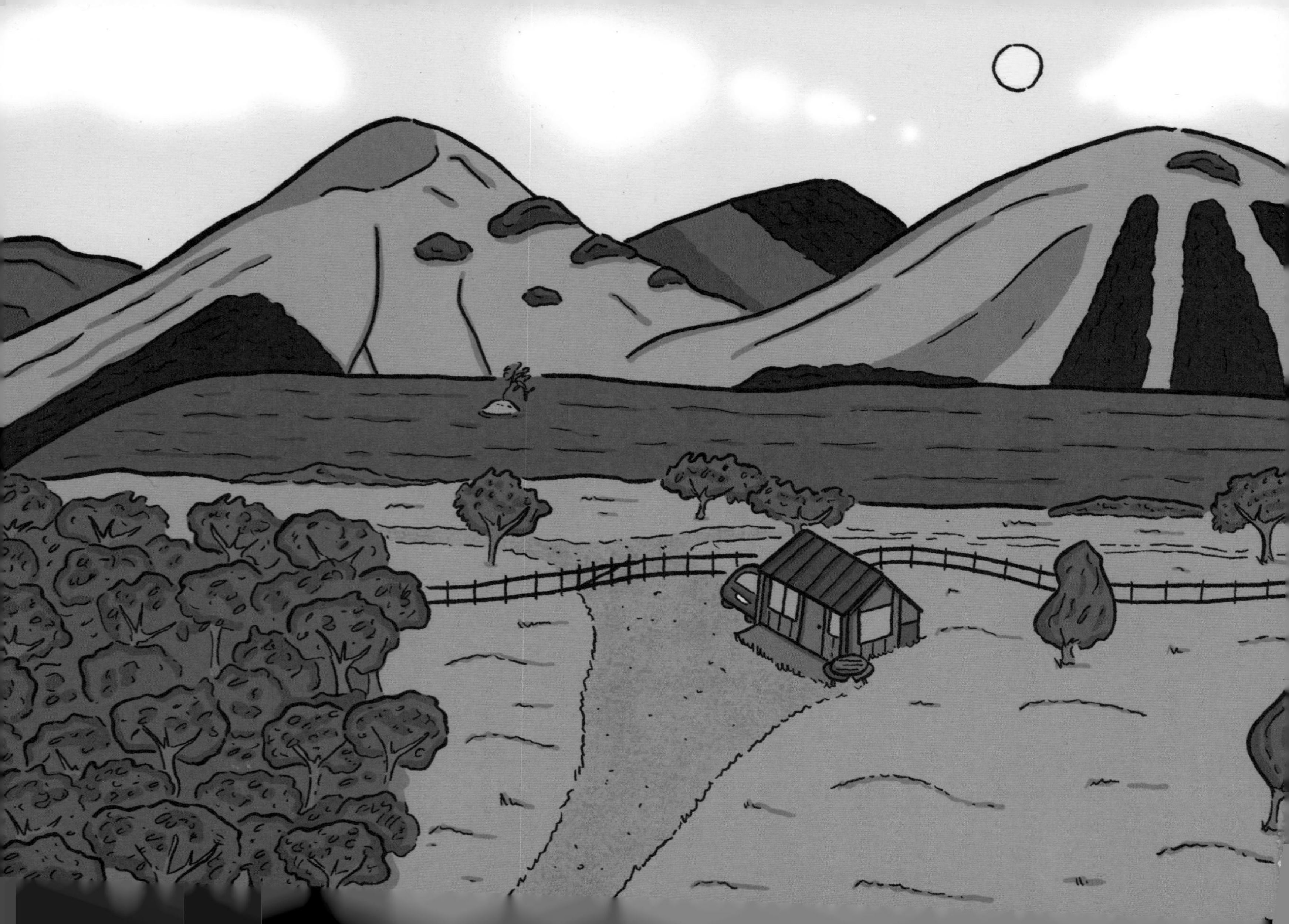